BATTLING THE COMMANDER

Battling the
Commander

LEFT BEHIND
>THE KIDS<

Jerry B. Jenkins

Tim LaHaye

WITH CHRIS FABRY

TYNDALE
KIDS

TYNDALE HOUSE PUBLISHERS, INC.
WHEATON, ILLINOIS

Visit Tyndale's exciting Web site at www.tyndale.com

Discover the latest Left Behind news at www.leftbehind.com

Published in association with the literary agency of Alive Communications, Inc., 7680 Goddard Street, Suite 200, Colorado Springs, CO 80920.

Edited by Curtis H. C. Lundgren

ISBN 0-8423-4296-6

Printed in the United States of America

08 07 06 05 04 03 02 01
 9   8   7   6   5   4   3   2   1

To Tim, Lisa, Meredith, and Ryan

TABLE OF CONTENTS

What's Gone On Before

JUDD Thompson Jr. and the rest of the Young
Tribulation Force are in danger. Global
Community Commander Blancka and
Morale Monitors Felicia and Melinda are
after Judd and his friend Vicki Byrne.

When Judd and Vicki are swept into a
river, a GC helicopter captures Vicki, but
Judd escapes.

While most of the Young Trib Force meet
in the underground hideout at the Stahley
mansion, Vicki is questioned by the Global
Community. Mitchell Stein, a Jewish busi-
nessman friend, helps her plead her case
before Commander Blancka. Before the
commander can make a decision about
Vicki's fate, Lionel Washington and his friend
Conrad Graham whisk Vicki away from the
GC jail. Conrad remains with the GC as
Lionel rushes Vicki to the hideout.

Not knowing Lionel's plan, Darrion
Stahley attempts her own rescue of Vicki and

is caught by the GC. The next morning, Conrad and Mr. Stein are suspected in Vicki's disappearance.

The kids must decide whether to run, hide, or face their enemy.

ONE

The Suspects

THE newest member of the Young Tribulation Force shook his head as Morale Monitor Melinda accused him of working against the Global Community.

They don't know where Vicki and Lionel are, Conrad Graham thought as Commander Blancka fumed.

"You helped Vicki escape," Melinda said, still groggy from sleeping pills Lionel had given her the night before.

"You're crazy," Conrad said. "You and Lionel blew that. I told you questioning her was a bad idea!"

"That was part of your plan," Melinda said.

The commander interrupted. "Graham, tell me about the call."

"Some guy said you wanted to see

Melinda," Conrad said. "I just delivered the message."

"You didn't verify it?"

"There was no reason," Conrad said. "Besides, everything's been crazy around here."

"He knows something and he's not telling," Felicia said.

Conrad turned on her. "How do we know Melinda didn't set this up with Lionel? Ask her what she was doing in that cell—"

"Lionel drugged her!" Felicia said.

"Enough," Commander Blancka said, glaring at Conrad. "Until I sort this out, you'll stay locked up like Stein."

"But, sir—"

"Take him away!"

Judd and the others inspected the underground hangar and found scattered rocks and dirt. Airplane equipment lay strewn about.

Mark pointed out the steel girders. "That's why we're safe here," he said.

Judd found the wall the GC had cut through to get to him and Ryan. Plaster and flooring from above covered the hole.

"We have only one way in or out," Judd said, showing Mark the collapsed secret door in the hillside.

"We can dig a new opening," Mark said. "Won't be fancy, but we'll have another exit."

The kids grabbed tools. After a few minutes, Vicki threw down her shovel. "Have you guys forgotten Darrion and Conrad?" she said. "They're facing Blancka!"

"Darrion said the same thing about you," Judd said, "and look where she is now."

"At least she cared enough to do something," Vicki said.

"Don't give me that!" Judd shouted. "I risked my life to get back here."

"To do what?" Vicki said. "Save us?"

Mark and Shelly stopped digging.

"Settle down," Lionel said. "We're on the same side, remember?"

"Yeah, but Judd always has to show us who's boss," Vicki said.

Judd shook his head.

"The GC are going to figure out who Darrion is," Vicki said. "We have to get her out."

"They'll probably trace the cycle back here," Judd said. "That's why we're digging."

Vicki rolled her eyes. "My point exactly," she said. "You care more about yourself—"

"If Darrion had listened, she wouldn't be where she is."

"Like you've never made a mistake," Vicki said.

"Judd's right," Lionel said. "Conrad's our best bet to get her out."

"He might not even know they have her," Vicki said.

Judd reached for Vicki's shoulder, but she jerked away.

Lionel stared at them. "Is something going on here?"

Judd scratched his head. "Give us a minute."

Lionel returned to help Mark and Shelly.

"You're upset about Darrion," Judd said.

"That's not all," Vicki said. "We got out of there so fast there wasn't time to bring Phoenix."

"You're worried about a dog?"

"I promised Ryan. Maybe promises don't mean that much to you—"

"Stop it!" Judd said. "I know you promised, but risking your life for Phoenix doesn't make sense."

"You get mixed up with a biker gang and try to jump a motorcycle over a river, and I don't make sense?"

Judd took Vicki by the shoulders. "This is partly because of us."

Vicki squinted. "Don't flatter yourself!"

"I care for you, Vicki, but—"

4

"Get this," she interrupted. "I don't go for arrogant types who think they're always right. If you want to be friends, fine. Other than that, no."

Conrad sat back against the cell door.

"Know anything about Vicki?" Mr. Stein said from the next cell. When Conrad hesitated, Mr. Stein added, "I only want to know that she is safe."

"If the GC don't know where she is, she's OK," Conrad said.

Mr. Stein sighed. "You are one of them, are you not?"

"What do you mean?"

Mr. Stein told his story. His wife and daughter Chaya had believed Jesus was the Messiah before Chaya was killed in the earthquake. Mr. Stein had laughed at them. "Now I'm not so sure they were wrong. I read a part of the New Testament last night, plus some of Tsion Ben-Judah's Web site."

"The Web site got me too," Conrad said. "Then Judd and Vicki explained it, and it all came together."

"I do not know what to believe," Mr. Stein said. "I have so many questions."

Conrad inched closer to the bars. "I don't know that much, but like what?"

"All right," Mr. Stein said, "if Jesus really is the Messiah, how could he forgive someone who has been against him all his life?"

"That's me too," Conrad said.

"But—," Mr. Stein said. "I am a Jew who rejected his Messiah. And the way I treated Chaya! Surely God could not forgive such an offense."

"There are stories in the Bible about people who turned around," Conrad said.

"That is not my only problem," Mr. Stein said. "If this is all true, God has caused millions to die or suffer."

"I don't think he's mean," Conrad said. "I think he's trying to get our attention."

"But there's another problem. If my wife and daughter were right, Nicolae Carpathia is the Antichrist. With all the good he has done, how can I believe that?"

A guard came and took Mr. Stein away. A few minutes later another prisoner was led in. Conrad peered through the dim light to see who it was.

Vicki retreated to a corner. She was crushed but didn't want anyone to know. She had hoped Judd had feelings for her, and several times he had started to say something but never finished. Under the desk in the rubble of New Hope Village Church, she felt close to him. But now he had changed, and Vicki felt foolish.

Shelly came and sat next to Vicki. "Mark punched through the dirt wall about half an hour ago, no thanks to you."

"Sorry."

"What's up?"

Vicki shook her head.

Judd sat by what was left of the Stahley's pool, throwing in clods of dirt and watching them break apart. He wanted to tell Vicki how he felt, but it was clear her feelings weren't as strong as his.

Evening shadows stretched across the Stahley property.

Vicki is too young anyway, Judd thought. But her angry words had hurt him. They had been through so much together. And now this.

Something caught Judd's eye at the edge of the woods. Branches moved and leaves rustled. He sat still. The sounds stopped. Judd relaxed. Then came the squawk of a radio. He dropped and crawled toward the house. Inside, he moved to the window. Nothing.

He quietly called Lionel and told him to watch the other side of the house. Suddenly, Judd spotted two uniformed GC officers heading toward them and more scattered in the woods. A helicopter flew overhead.

Lionel ran to Judd. "How could I have been so stupid!"

"What?" Judd said.

"My radio! It has a homing device. I led them right to us!"

Conrad motioned to Darrion. She seemed to recognize him but looked cautious. Conrad pulled back his hair and showed the mark on his forehead. "Do they know who you are?" he said.

Darrion shook her head. "The commander kept saying he couldn't place me. I said I was Laura Grover and that I'd found the motorcycle in a big house. I have to figure a way out of here," Darrion said.

"Hang tight," Conrad said. "They might turn you loose in a few days."

"And if they figure out who I am?"

"Then I'll have to get us both out."

Vicki and Shelly ran to the others when they heard the commotion.

Mark said, "The GC is tracking Lionel's radio. Be ready to run."

Vicki frowned. "Give me the radio."

Lionel handed it to her. "I hope you know what you're doing."

TWO

Shelly's Trick

JUDD and Lionel helped Mark brace the new exit so it wouldn't cave in. The opening was the size of a window.

Mark stuck his head through the opening. "GC is almost to the house. And they're armed to the teeth."

Judd ran to the computer room. *I gotta get Vicki and Shelly out of there!*

"Are you up for this?" Vicki said.

"This is my acting debut," Shelly said. "Get that picture over the entrance so they don't find you guys."

Judd hurried in. "We have to get out of here now," he said.

11

"Help me get this picture in place," Vicki said.

Judd pulled out Conrad's gun. "You don't understand—they're almost inside!"

"Help me!" she said.

Judd grabbed the picture, and something cracked. The picture fell.

"Someone's in there," came a voice.

"Hold it in place," Vicki whispered.

"Let's go now," Lionel said.

"What about Judd?" Mark said.

"Do what you want," Lionel said. "I'm heading for the woods."

Mark moved through the opening, but before Lionel could follow, Mark scampered back inside. Lionel heard chopper blades. When the helicopter flew toward the river, Lionel followed Mark outside. They crawled to a small hill. They tucked their arms close to their bodies and rolled to the bottom, then crouched and hurried into a wooded area.

When they stopped to catch their breath, Mark said, "No way Judd can hold them off."

Lionel backtracked and found a drainpipe in a clump of bushes. He pulled out his flashlight and peered inside.

"Judd said there was a landing strip somewhere near here."

The helicopter grew louder.

Vicki heard crunching glass coming from the kitchen. The helicopter hovered, then flew away. Vicki gasped at the click of a rifle.

"Oh, hi there," Shelly said.

"Hands in the air now!" a man shouted.

"What do you want with me?"

"On the floor!"

"You don't have to be so mean," Shelly said. "I just took some crackers."

"Where are the others?"

"Others?"

"The radio!" a man shouted. "It gave you away."

Shelly said, "You can have that thing. I don't want it."

"Where did you get it?"

Shelly filled her mouth with crackers. "This black kid comes up and asks if I'm hungry," she said. "He could tell I was. So he says he'll tell me where to get some food if I do him a favor."

"Washington, sir?" a man said.

"Yeah, let her keep going."

"There's not much more," Shelly said. "He

said if I'd take his radio and keep it until somebody found me, he'd tell me where I could get something to eat. Crackers is all I found."

"Was there anyone with him?" a man said.

"A girl," Shelly said. "Redhead. Scrawny."

"Exactly where?" a man said.

"Across the river," Shelly said. "They headed south or west, whatever's away from the river."

Someone radioed the chopper.

"What do we do with the girl?" another said.

"I'll see what Blancka says," the leader said.

Vicki's arms were tired from holding the picture in place.

The chopper blew sticks and leaves into the drainpipe. Lionel and Mark crept deeper into the pipe, a trickle of water rushing past their feet.

"Hope there's no snakes," Mark said.

"Better snakes than the GC," Lionel said.

The boys moved deeper until they could barely hear the chopper. In several places, the earthquake had crinkled the pipe.

"We'd better turn back," Mark said. "We're not gonna find anything."

Lionel heard fluttering wings. "Get down!" he yelled as bats flew past. Lionel shuddered, but he was curious about what might be ahead. They came to a break where dirt blocked their way. The earthquake had opened a hole in the pipe. "Look at this!" Lionel said.

A natural cave stretched several hundred feet.

Judd struggled to hold the picture. He wished Vicki would rest so she could return the favor.

The GC leader sent others searching throughout the house. Judd heard the man talking on his radio in the next room.

Judd told Vicki, "I don't think I can hold this anymore."

Vicki closed her eyes. "We have to."

The painting slipped and banged against the floor. Judd massaged his arms and bent double from exhaustion.

"Did you hear that?" the leader said.

Shelly said, "Stuff's been falling since I got here. The earthquake, you know."

Someone knocked on the wall, and a knife sliced through the picture of the Stahleys. Judd and Vicki squeezed to the side as a flashlight came through.

"Anything?" the leader said.

"Lotsa dust."

The flashlight scanned back and forth as Judd leaned out of its beam.

Shelly screamed. The light went away.

"I saw someone out there!"

The leader took several men and bolted out the front door toward the driveway. Judd propped the picture up as best he could.

"You guys better leave now," Shelly whispered.

"Not without you," Vicki said.

"They'll know something's up. Go!"

Judd and Vicki slipped into the underground computer room. They looked for Lionel and Mark in the hangar.

Lionel and Mark took ten minutes to break through the dirt and rock. When they finally pulled themselves inside the cave, Lionel gave a low whistle. "It's huge."

The cave was twenty feet high. The floor was rocky but fairly level and dry.

"This would make a great hideout," Lionel said.

"Sure," Mark said. "No food, no heat. Just like home."

Lionel noticed a small beam of light coming from the back of the cave. Mark helped him reach a ledge, and Lionel pulled himself up.

Lionel said, "This could be another entrance."

"No tree roots," Mark said. "We may be right under that landing strip. One good jolt and the whole thing could come down on us."

Judd was alone when Lionel and Mark returned that evening. "The GC bought Shelly's story," he said. "Took the radio and told her to get to a shelter before she gets shot for looting. They headed for the river, but we'd better not risk staying here long."

Lionel told Judd about the cave.

"Let's check it out after dark," Judd said.

Conrad was fascinated by Darrion's story. She had gone from having everything she wanted to having nothing.

"I shouldn't have tried to rescue Vicki," Darrion said. She put her head against the bars. "God didn't seem interested in us, so I tried something on my own."

The door opened and Mr. Stein was led back to his cell.

"They still suspect me," Mr. Stein whispered after the guard left. He rubbed his forehead. "I wish I could talk to Vicki."

"If they suspect you, they might let me go," Conrad said. "Then I could help you both escape."

"They will not let the girl go," Mr. Stein said. "They know who she is."

"Vicki?" Darrion said.

"No, *you*, my dear. They suspect the others are at your house. One group has already been there and gone. They are sending another group tonight."

THREE

The Cave

WHILE he ate, Lionel walked through the hangar and gathered supplies. He found a long piece of rope and a metal hook strong enough to hold his weight. He nailed together five other pieces of wood, then screwed the hook in the middle.

"What's that?" Shelly said.

"You'll see tonight," Lionel said.

Lionel looked over Judd's shoulder and read the computer screen. Judd had pulled up Tsion Ben-Judah's Web site. A fast-moving number on the edge of the screen showed how many people were logging on.

"That can't be right," Lionel said. "The numbers are going by too fast."

"I've never seen anything like it either," Judd said.

Judd had logged on to download a Bible, but he found himself distracted by the Web site. He felt guilty for how little he was studying. He knew devotions weren't possible when you were running from the Global Community. Still, he wanted to stay "in the Word" like Bruce had taught them.

From the moment Judd had prayed to receive Christ, he felt hungry for the Bible. He wanted to know all the things he had missed the first time. He wrote verses on scraps of paper and tucked them inside his pockets.

But after Bruce had died, no one checked on him or asked him how things were going. Slowly, with all he had to do, he found it easy to let it slide.

As Judd looked over the message on Tsion's Web site, he wondered who else might be reading it. Perhaps members of the 144,000 witnesses. Perhaps Nicolae Carpathia himself. His friend in New Babylon, Pavel, had told him Nicolae checked Tsion's Web site frequently.

If he's reading this, Judd thought, *he has to be seething.* Judd read:

> Good day to you, my dear brother or sister in the Lord. I come to you with a

heart both heavy with sorrow and yet full of joy. I sorrow personally over the loss of my wife and teenagers. I mourn for so many who have died since the coming of Christ to rapture his church. I mourn for mothers all over the globe who lost their children. And I weep for a world that has lost an entire generation.

How strange to not see the smiling faces or hear the laughter of children. As much as we enjoyed them, we could not have known how much they taught us and how much they added to our lives until they were gone.

I am also sad because the great earthquake appears to have snuffed out 25 percent of the remaining population. For generations people have called natural disasters "acts of God." This is not so. Ages ago, God the Father gave Satan, the prince and power of the air, control of Earth's weather. God allowed destruction and death by natural causes, yes, because of the fall of man. And no doubt God at times intervened against such actions by the evil one because of the prayers of his people.

Tsion went on to say the recent earthquake was an act of God necessary to fulfill prophecy and get the attention of those who don't believe in Jesus. He said he was amazed at the work of the Global Community in setting up communications so quickly. But Tsion said he was shocked at what he saw in the media.

"Do they still have a television around here?" Lionel said.

"Maybe in one of the bedrooms upstairs," Judd said.

Judd continued reading. Tsion grieved the way society had forgotten God at a time when they needed him most.

> If you believe in Jesus Christ as the only Son of God the Father, you are against everything taught by Enigma Babylon.
>
> There are those who ask, why not cooperate? Why not be loving and accepting? Loving we are. Accepting we cannot be.
>
> Enigma Babylon does not believe in the one true God. It believes in any god, or no god, or god as a concept. There is no right or wrong. The self is the center of this man-made religion.
>
> My challenge to you today is to choose up sides. Join a team. If one side is right, the other is wrong. We cannot both be right.

But I do not call you to a life of ease. During the next five years before the glorious return of Christ to set up his kingdom on earth, three-fourths of the population that was left after the Rapture will die. In the meantime, we should invest our lives in the cause. A great missionary martyr of the twentieth century named Jim Elliot is credited with saying this: "He is no fool who gives up what he cannot keep [this temporal life] to gain what he cannot lose [eternal life with Christ]."

And now a word to my fellow converted Jews from each of the twelve tribes: Plan on rallying in Jerusalem a month from today as we seek the great soul harvest that is ours to gather.

And now unto him who is able to keep you from falling, to Christ, that great shepherd of the sheep, be power and dominion and glory now and forevermore, world without end, Amen. Your servant, Tsion Ben-Judah.

Lionel returned with a small television. Judd watched him flick through channels. Before the Rapture Judd had seen things he knew his parents wouldn't have liked, but nothing compared to this.

One game show allowed the winner to kill the other contestant. The next channel showed the torture and murder of innocent people. On another, a séance was performed as people tried to communicate with the dead. Enigma Babylon approved of an educational program that taught viewers how to cast spells on enemies. As Lionel flicked the stations, things got worse.

"Turn it off," Judd said.

"Dr. Ben-Judah was right," Lionel said. "This is the bottom."

Conrad explained his plan. Darrion and Mr. Stein agreed to help.

"I just wish I could talk to Vicki again," Mr. Stein said. "I keep thinking about what she and Chaya said to me. I can believe that Jesus was a great man. A good teacher. Even a prophet. But I am still not sure about him actually being God."

Darrion said, "Why would you call him a good teacher if he told a lie?"

"I don't understand," Mr. Stein said.

"Jesus said a lot of good things," Darrion continued. "Be kind to your neighbor. Do to others what you would have them do to you. But he also said he *was* God. So if you think he was just a good man, you call him a liar."

"I did not say that."

"Saying you're God is crazy, unless it's true," Darrion said. "If he was insane, he's nobody you'd want to follow."

Mr. Stein sighed.

"What she's saying is right," Conrad said. "Jesus taught great things and claimed to be the Son of God. Then he backed that up by doing miracles. Even coming back from the dead. If that doesn't prove he was who he said he was, nothing will convince you."

Mr. Stein put his face in his hands. "The weight I feel is immense. If you are right, I have rejected the Holy One, and I haven't believed my own flesh and blood."

Darrion came close to the bars. "Vicki told me Chaya prayed for you every day. You don't have to feel guilty. She only wanted you to believe."

As night approached, Lionel gathered his materials and went to meet with the others. He found Vicki alone. "You want to talk about it?" he said.

Vicki shook her head.

Judd called them together and went over the plan.

"If we have to move, why don't we take all our stuff now?" Shelly said.

"We want to be sure this cave won't collapse," Judd said. "We don't want to lose any of our supplies."

As they left, Mark backtracked and tied a string across the patio doorway to the mansion. He ran it outside to a pane of glass perched above the concrete.

Lionel led the way. Mark helped him carry the equipment that would lower them into the cave. The ground was spongy and filled with crickets.

Judd held the flashlight and searched for the opening as they walked. After several minutes, Mark suggested they go through the drainpipe.

Judd held up a hand. "Hold on," he said.

Looking closely, Lionel spied a hole about the size of a fist surrounded by grass and rocks. Judd and Mark dug out the hole to about three feet in diameter.

Lionel wedged the boards between two rocks and let the rope down. Judd went first and shinnied into the cavern. His voice echoed as he called out, "You guys were right. This is perfect."

Lionel covered the door he had made with

mud and grass. He dug out a landing where the kids could climb and then push the door open. When he had finished, he covered the area with extra dirt and a few small rocks.

"How's it look?" Lionel said.

"You'd never know it was there," Vicki said.

A crash behind Lionel sent him to the ground. "What was that?"

"What I was afraid of," Mark said. "Company. Somebody tripped the wire."

Lionel heard a sound that gave him chills. Dogs.

Conrad watched Mr. Stein. He seemed to be in pain. A guard unlocked Darrion's cell.

"What's going on?" she said.

"We know who you are," the guard said. "Commander wants to see you. They're gonna catch those other two tonight."

"I don't know what you're talking about," Darrion said.

"Sir, tell Commander Blancka it worked," Conrad said.

The guard turned and eyed Conrad.

"Tell him I did what he wanted," Conrad said. "I got the information."

"Of all the dirty tricks!" Mr. Stein screamed.

"You said you were one of us," Darrion said.

"And you were foolish enough to believe me," Conrad said.

The guard looked confused. Mr. Stein grabbed Conrad's shirt and banged him against the cell bars.

"Let him go, now!" the guard shouted.

"Don't trust this little weasel!" Mr. Stein shouted.

"I said, let him go!" The guard pulled his nightstick. Mr. Stein turned Conrad loose.

"I'll report this to the commander," the guard said.

"Just hurry up," Conrad gasped.

Darrion winced when the guard pulled her through the door.

"I did not hurt you badly, did I?" Mr. Stein whispered after they were gone.

Conrad smiled. "Don't worry about it. I'm just a weasel. Where'd you come up with that?"

"Probably the movies I watched when I was younger," Mr. Stein said. "We must pray your plan works."

"Pray?" Conrad said.

"Pray to the God of my fathers, Abraham, Isaac, and Jacob. And pray to the Son of God himself, Jesus Christ."

"Then you believe?" Conrad said.

"My daughter was right. I believe Jesus is the only way and that I cannot come to God except through him."

Conrad smiled.

"I am ashamed to have been so blind," Mr. Stein said. "Chaya's last moments were spent trying to tell me the truth, but I would not listen."

"I can help you with the prayer, if you'd like," Conrad said.

Mr. Stein nodded.

"Just ask God to forgive you for the wrong stuff you've done. Tell him you're sorry for not believing sooner."

Mr. Stein prayed.

"Now tell him you believe that Jesus died for you and rose again. Tell God you don't trust in anything you've done, but only what Jesus has done. Ask him to be your Savior and Lord."

Tearfully, Mr. Stein completed his prayer. "Oh God, please forgive me," he cried. "Come into my life."

Vicki broke into a sweat when she heard the dogs.

"What's going on?" Judd shouted from below.

"Quiet!" Vicki said.

"Everybody in," Lionel said. "We don't have time to figure out who it is."

"What if it's Conrad and Darrion?" Vicki said.

"With dogs?" Lionel said. "No way."

"Get in the cave," Shelly said as she took off for the house.

"What is she doing?" Lionel said.

Lionel helped Vicki onto the rope. She was nervous about climbing that far. When she got to the bottom, she put a hand on Judd's shoulder. "Shelly will be all right. She can do it."

FOUR

Conrad and the Commander

THE next morning a different guard returned for Conrad. Darrion had been gone all night.

"Don't believe anything he says," Mr. Stein yelled as the man led Conrad away.

Melinda and Felicia waited outside the interview room and scowled when Conrad sat beside them.

"I wanted to tell you guys what was up, but I didn't want to blow my cover," Conrad said.

"What are you talking about?" Melinda said.

"The commander put me down there so I could listen to those two talk," he said. "I got what he wanted."

"I don't believe you," Felicia said. "You're one of them."

"I was just as surprised as you when Lionel turned up dirty."

The girls turned away.

"I need your help," Conrad said, moving where he could see them. "I'm going to catch Lionel, the girl, and that other guy."

The door opened. Commander Blancka came outside. "What is this, Graham?"

"Commander, sir, I figured since I was innocent, you put me in with the others to spy. It worked."

The commander cleared his throat. "I didn't. I mean . . . what did you find out?"

"Darrion's definitely one of them, sir," Conrad said.

"We've had someone talking to her all night," the commander said. "She says she doesn't know them."

"If it's all right with you, I'd like to see the look on her face when I tell you the whole story," Conrad said.

The commander motioned the three inside. Darrion looked exhausted. Her eyes were puffy and red. *The commander probably talked about her parents*, Conrad thought.

Conrad knew this would be the tough part. If he could convince the commander he wasn't partners with the others, he had a chance to get Darrion and Mr. Stein out.

Vicki was worried when she awoke and Shelly hadn't returned. She felt stiff and sore from sleeping on the cave floor. In the light of the embers from Judd's fire, she crept to the other side to inspect the drainpipe. Vicki hadn't told anyone, but she was scared she wouldn't be able to climb the rope that led out of the cave. Coming down wasn't so bad, but she had never been very good at climbing in gym class. She couldn't let anyone know. Especially Judd.

Vicki watched the trickling water go through the pipe and wondered how long they would have to be on the run. Staying in the cave wouldn't be bad if they had food and sleeping bags, but they had none.

Vicki looked at Judd. He was asleep. Part of her just wanted to get out and not have to deal with him anymore. He had yelled at Lionel for letting Shelly go. Vicki couldn't imagine being cooped up with him for a few days, but she couldn't imagine not having him around either.

Lionel stirred and saw Vicki. "She's not back yet?" he said.

Vicki shook her head. "I hope the GC didn't take her away."

"Judd was right. I should've stopped her."

"He was not right," Vicki said. "Shelly can take care of herself as well as anyone."

"What's going on between you and Judd?"

Vicki frowned. "Nothing. That's the problem. I thought he really cared for me but we're too far apart."

"You mean, you're from a trailer park and he's a rich kid?" Lionel said. "I'd say that's not much of an issue at the moment. You're both sleeping in a cave."

Vicki smiled. "It's not the time to let these feelings take over."

"I know one thing," Lionel said. "Judd cares a lot more than you think."

Vicki was startled by a *tick, tick* sound from the pipe behind her. Lionel craned his neck.

"You think we should wake Judd and Mark?" Vicki said.

Lionel shook his head. "I'll check it out."

Lionel returned a few minutes later carrying a blanket. Shelly was right behind him. Vicki gave her a hug and watched as Lionel opened the blanket on the floor. Inside were food, a few bottles of water, and the laptop computer from the hideout.

When Shelly caught her breath, she said, "I went to the front of the house. I figured if these were GC, they'd recognize me from before. They were GC all right, but a different group.

"I ran in the front and screamed. The guys about shot me! I told them you guys came back and held a gun on me."

"We're gettin' to be as mean as snakes," Lionel said.

"Don't say that," Shelly said. "I think I saw one as I came up the drainpipe."

Vicki shivered. "What happened next?"

"They asked which way you went, and I pointed toward the woods. They took their dogs down there but came back a few minutes later. Said they were going to stay all night and watch.

"I told them I wasn't going to let you two come back and get me, that I was going to stay with them. They searched the whole house but didn't find the hideout."

"How'd you get out?" Lionel said.

"I thought they'd leave, but they kept looking through their binoculars. I told 'em I was going to sleep and then head for a shelter at sunup."

"They bought it?" Lionel said.

"I guess," Shelly said. "They kept searching in the garage and near the patio. That's where the dogs kept going."

Judd awakened and welcomed Shelly.

"When they took the dogs upstairs, I slipped behind the picture and into the hide-out. I figured Judd could use the computer. I hope it's charged up."

Judd picked up the laptop and inspected it. "Good thinking."

"I came back upstairs and pretended to sleep," Shelly said. "I remembered Mark talking about another entrance to the pipe."

"Are you sure nobody saw you?" Judd said.

"Don't think so," Shelly said.

"You could have led them right to us," Judd said.

"She just saved us!" Vicki screamed, waking Mark. "If she hadn't gone back there, the GC would have tracked us down for sure."

Vicki's voice echoed through the cave. Then came barking.

"Come on," Lionel said. "We have to block the drain!"

"I heard everything," Conrad said, looking straight at Darrion. "She tried to get Stein to be a part of their group."

"What group is that?" the commander said.

"Some religious order," Conrad said. "They go around with stuff on their foreheads."

The commander looked at Darrion. "I don't see anything," he said.

Conrad laughed. "They claim it's invisible."

Melinda and Felicia chuckled.

"Darrion tried to convince the guy, but he wouldn't budge. She told him Judd and Vicki had gone to her house, then went back to the basement of their church."

The commander scribbled notes on a pad.

"You lying double-crosser!" Darrion shouted.

"You're the liar," Conrad said as a guard subdued Darrion.

"What about Washington?" the commander said.

"I'm afraid he's one of them too," Conrad said. "Lionel planned to get Vicki out all along. I should have seen it."

"And Stein?"

"From what I picked up, Vicki was a friend of his family. He's misguided but not guilty of anything."

The commander nodded and whispered to a guard.

"Commander, I don't like this," Felicia

said. "From the time Lionel and Conrad met those other two—"

"I appreciate your concern," Commander Blancka said, "but this is valuable information. Go back to the church and search every inch. I want Washington back here to stand—"

The commander's radio squawked. He excused himself, then called Conrad, Felicia, and Melinda into another room.

"Looks like they were at this Stahley girl's house last night," the commander said. "We've got a team waiting in case they come back. I'll assign backup. My guess is you'll find them at this church."

Judd and the others dug furiously. They filled the pipe with dirt and rocks. The dogs barked at the end of the tunnel. When the entrance was blocked, Judd stayed close. The others prepared to leave.

The dogs pawed at the earth on the other side. Two men caught up to them. One cursed. "They must have stayed right here last night."

"Probably took off with the other girl," another said.

The dogs were back at the dirt again, and Judd heard one yelp. The two men left.

"Looks like we're safe for a while," Judd told the others.

Judd asked Lionel to carefully look from the top entrance. Lionel climbed the rope with ease and lifted the opening a few inches. He slid back down and sat by Vicki.

"They're headed back to the house," Lionel said.

Judd opened the laptop while the others ate breakfast. The battery was almost dead.

"We'll only have one shot to see our messages," Judd said.

"You don't have a phone line," Vicki said.

"This works on a regular line and it also has a sat-phone built in," Judd said. He dialed up and logged onto his E-mail. There were hundreds of messages forwarded from Tsion Ben-Judah's Web site. Judd scrolled down the list. A small screen popped up, saying the battery was running out.

Judd scanned the messages and recognized one with a Global Community address. It was from Conrad.

As he opened the message, the laptop went blank.

Judd pounded the floor of the cave.

"What did it say?" Vicki said.

Judd shook his head. "Couldn't read it.

Maybe Conrad got Darrion out. Maybe he's in trouble and needs our help."

"We could sneak back up to the house and try to recharge it," Mark said.

"Too risky," Judd said. "But at some point we'll need to communicate with the outside."

"There's gotta be someone who can help us," Mark said.

"There's always your friend with the motorcycle," Vicki smirked.

Judd stared off but didn't say a word.

FIVE

Lionel's Run

Two days later, Judd knew the kids were desperate. The GC hadn't discovered them, but they had no food and only the water from the dripping drain. They had tried to keep the fire going, but they were running out of fuel.

"Somebody's going to have to get some wood," Lionel said.

"Won't do any good," Judd said. "No matches."

Shelly put her head on a rock and held her stomach.

"We have to get supplies and recharge this battery," Judd said.

"Maybe they've pulled out," Mark said.

"Wouldn't bet on it," Lionel said. "Probably at least one guard will stay behind for a few days."

"How about digging into the back entrance at night?" Shelly said.

"They'd spot us," Judd said.

"Then we have to create a diversion," Lionel said. He drew a plan in the dirt. One of them would go in for supplies.

"There won't be time to recharge the computer," Judd said.

"Then whoever goes in stays all night. We come back the next night to get him."

"Him?" Vicki said.

"Or her," Lionel said.

"We could just make a run for it," Mark said.

"I know how these guys operate," Lionel said. "They've got a net out for us. They'll be waiting."

The kids agreed to chance the nighttime break-in.

"Who goes?" Lionel said.

"I'm the one who knows the place the best," Judd said.

"We'll draw straws," Vicki said.

Mark held up five splinters of wood. When they had drawn, Lionel held the shortest.

Conrad showed a picture of Lionel and Vicki to a worker at a shelter. The worker shook his head. "Haven't seen them," he said.

42

Melinda and Felicia joined Conrad. "Any luck?" he said.

The girls shook their heads. "I don't want to go back to the commander and say we've spent two days and have nothing to show for it," Melinda said.

"We could try the high school again," Conrad said.

Felicia frowned. "Like it or not, we'd better head back. Our meeting's in a half hour."

Conrad had tried not to be too friendly with the girls. He wanted them to believe he was on their side, but he didn't want to act like fast pals. Conrad could sense that the girls still distrusted him. At times they whispered to each other. He had read somewhere in the Bible that he was supposed to do good to his enemies, but he didn't know what that meant to people like Felicia and Melinda.

Conrad wanted to talk with Mr. Stein. The commander had released him two days earlier, but a guard was secretly watching the man's house. Conrad feared Mr. Stein might still have questions or doubts. Or he might have changed his mind about Jesus. Conrad had seen the mark on the man's forehead, but he wasn't sure if a person could un-pray a prayer. He couldn't wait to see Judd again. He had a million questions.

Conrad hoped to slip past the guard and visit Mr. Stein late that night, assuming he could get away without Melinda or Felicia seeing him.

Conrad was also concerned about Darrion. He knew the commander had withheld food and water from her. The GC's efforts hadn't worked. But how long could she hold out? Conrad tried to slip her a bottle of water before they met with the commander, but Melinda and Felicia stayed close.

"We've been to fourteen shelters in the area, sir," Conrad told the commander. "Some of them twice. The hospitals haven't treated anyone fitting their description. We found the location of the Washington and Thompson homes and checked there. The Byrne girl was staying with a pastor. The church is empty."

The commander grunted.

"He was killed at the start of the war," Conrad continued, "and it looks like this Byrne took in a bunch of kids. There's nothing left of that house."

"People don't just disappear," Commander Blancka said.

"Heard anything from the Stahley girl's house?" Melinda said.

The commander shook his head. "We've still got guards there, but I don't think they'll come back. My guess is they've found a place they think is safe, and they hope we'll forget about them." The commander looked out the window. "Well, I'm not going to forget. These kids have caused a lot of trouble. The top brass is watching. The whole Morale Monitor program could hinge on what happens here."

"We'll do all we can, sir," Felicia said.

The commander stared at the kids. "We'll break this Stahley girl soon. She has to talk. We'll find the others and make an example of them."

At dinner, Conrad excused himself. He had written a note to Darrion earlier in the day. It read, *You and the others are alive as long as you hold out. Don't give up. I'll try to get you some water tonight.* He put a rubber band around the note and attached it to a candy bar.

He darted behind the former police station. Darrion was in the farthest cell down the hall, and she was the only prisoner. He put his hand through the window and rattled the wrapper. Darrion looked up. Conrad put a finger to his lips. He threw the candy bar as hard as he could and watched it skid to a stop a few feet from Darrion's cell.

Darrion used her blanket to pull the candy closer until she reached it. She ate it hungrily as she read the note. When she was finished, she mouthed, "Thank you," then licked the wrapper.

As Conrad raced back to the tent to finish his dinner, a light rain began to fall.

"What took you so long?" Felicia said suspiciously.

"If you have to know, I got some bad water," Conrad said, taking two bottles from the table. "I've been—"

"That's enough," Melinda said. "Not at dinner."

Conrad shrugged. "You asked."

Melinda leaned close. "You feel up to a little nighttime investigating?"

"Sure, where you going?"

"We're gonna hit that Stein guy," Felicia said. "We've got a hunch he has those kids hidden somewhere."

Conrad's eyes widened. "They could have gone there before we put the guard on him. Where's he live, anyway?"

"His house is demolished," Melinda said. "And his daughter died in the earthquake. He's living at his office in Barrington. We leave at midnight."

Lionel asked Judd for his E-mail password, and Judd scribbled it on a scrap of paper.

"Look at all you want," Judd said, "but you'll have to go through a lot of forwarded messages from Tsion."

Judd explained how to recharge the laptop, then said, "If you'd rather I go—"

"Oh no, you don't," Vicki said. "Besides, Lionel knows as much about computers as you do."

Judd shook his head as Vicki walked away. "She hates me," he said.

"I don't think so," Lionel said. "You guys can work out whatever's come between you."

Judd changed the subject. "I can't remember, but there might be a battery backup in the desk. If you find one, make sure you—"

"I'll charge it up," Lionel said. "Are you looking for any special E-mails other than Conrad's?"

"His is most important," Judd said. "Write Tsion and tell him to pray."

Lionel climbed the rope and peeked through the entrance. It was raining harder, and water was leaking through the hatch.

"The rain's good for us," Judd said when Lionel returned. "I don't think the dogs can follow as well."

"How much food and water do you want?" Lionel said.

"As much as you can carry," Judd said.

Conrad met Melinda and Felicia near the jail. The girls had signed out a jeep from the commander. The rain was coming down hard as they started toward Barrington.

"Got an idea," Conrad said. "I brought a disk with me to do a data dump from the guy's computer. He might have some information stored."

"Good," Felicia said.

Melinda drove cautiously. Some of the main roads had been bulldozed and were easy to pass. Others were still in rough shape.

The kids were stopped twice at GC checkpoints. When the guards saw they were Morale Monitors, they waved them through.

A light was on upstairs at Mr. Stein's office. Melinda and Felicia walked across the street and found a man watching the building.

"What did he say?" Conrad said when the two returned.

"We're cool," Melinda said. "The guy radioed his buddy around back to watch for anyone trying to sneak out."

Conrad thought it odd that there were two guards and that the one in front hadn't questioned the girls further. Melinda tried the door. To Conrad's surprise, it was unlocked. The girls pulled out their guns.

"Maybe he's expecting us," Conrad whispered.

The office was dark. Conrad shone his flashlight around the room. There were several desks with computers. Some were on the floor. The walls of the building looked stable, though other buildings on the street had collapsed. They found Mr. Stein sleeping upstairs on a couch, an open Bible on the man's stomach.

That's a good sign, Conrad thought.

Melinda nodded toward the computer. Conrad waved them back outside.

"If we wake him up, he might alert the others," Conrad said. "I'll get on the computer while you guys check downstairs. Maybe there's some kind of basement where they're hiding."

Conrad pulled a disk from his pocket. When he was sure the girls were gone, he crept to the couch and gently shook Mr. Stein awake.

Conrad put a hand over the man's mouth and whispered, "You have to be quiet. Two Morale Monitors are downstairs."

Mr. Stein nodded. Conrad took his hand away. Conrad was glad to see the mark of the true believer on Mr. Stein's forehead.

"Is anyone hiding here?"

"No," Mr. Stein said. "How is Darrion?"

"Hungry," Conrad said, "but there's no time to talk. I'm loading a message on your computer. It has Judd's E-mail address. Follow the instructions I give and we might be able to get Darrion out alive."

Mr. Stein nodded.

"It's embedded in a file called *Chaya*," Conrad said. "I thought that would be easy for you to remember."

Mr. Stein smiled.

"Now go back to sleep and don't wake up until those two come back," Conrad said.

Conrad put the file onto Mr. Stein's hard drive, then erased the file from his own disk. He began copying files from the computer, but soon realized many of them were from Tsion Ben-Judah's Web site.

I can't let them see this! Conrad thought.

Melinda and Felicia returned.

"Almost finished," Conrad whispered.

"Has he been awake?" Felicia said.

Conrad shook his head.

Felicia kicked the couch, and Mr. Stein jumped like he had just been awakened. "Where are you hiding them?" Felicia screamed.

"What?" Mr. Stein said.

Felicia put her gun to the man's head. "I said, where are you hiding them?"

"Go ahead and pull the trigger," Melinda said.

Lionel crouched by the bushes near the back patio. The rain was blinding. It was difficult to see even a few feet ahead. Lionel pushed the light on his watch. Three more minutes. He edged closer to the house. He kept the laptop under his shirt and hoped the rain wouldn't damage it. Lionel saw two glowing objects in the house.

As planned, at exactly midnight, Lionel heard the scream and the gunshot. Two dogs barked. Cigarettes fell to the floor. The front door opened. A man shouted orders into his radio.

Lionel ran into the kitchen and nearly lost his balance as his wet shoes hit the floor. He rounded the corner and made it to the slashed picture of the Stahley family.

Lionel moved the picture and climbed through the opening. He prayed Judd and Vicki would be able to get back to the cave in time.

SIX

Cave Danger

JUDD preferred to have Mark join him, but
Vicki insisted. The rain matted her hair. It
had been Vicki's idea to scream. Judd
thought her piercing wail would not only
alert the GC but also scare them.

Once Judd made sure the GC guards were
after them, they bolted toward the clearing.
The rain fell hard. Judd held up a hand to
block it. He saw Mark's signal in the distance,
a blinking flashlight.

Judd was right about the dogs. They
couldn't track as well in the rain. He heard
their yelping and turned. Two flashlights
scanned the bottom of the hill.

A few yards from the entrance to the cave,
Judd picked up the signal again. A flashlight
beam crossed their path. Judd's heart sank.

"There they are!" a man yelled.

Judd grabbed Vicki's arm and pulled her
away from the hideout.

"To the woods," Judd yelled over the noise of the rain.

Conrad's first instinct was to reach out and grab Felicia's gun, but something made him hold back. The two girls seemed icy cold.

Mr. Stein turned pale. "I don't know what you're talking about," he said.

Felicia gritted her teeth and pushed the gun harder against the man's scalp. "Where are you hiding them?"

"I told you, I haven't seen Vicki or any of the others since—"

"Just get it over with," Melinda said. She glanced at Conrad. "Or maybe he wants to do it."

Conrad understood. In the split second when Melinda caught his eye, he knew the two were trying to trap him. Perhaps they had the commander's approval. That was probably why the guard at the front hadn't put up a fight about them searching the place. The whole evening had been a test.

Conrad shrugged. "You know this isn't gonna look good," he said.

Felicia pulled the gun away slightly, and Mr. Stein took a breath.

"I don't care what you do to the guy,"

Conrad continued, "but it's clear the commander wants him watched. If you two off him, I don't think the commander will be happy. Like it or not, this guy might be our best shot at finding Lionel and the others." Conrad put the computer disk in his pocket. "It's up to you. I don't mind a little blood."

Felicia looked at Melinda and put the gun away. She pushed Mr. Stein back on the couch.

"The authorities will hear about this!" Mr. Stein yelled.

Conrad jumped on the man, pushing him hard into the wall. "We are the authorities!" he yelled.

Vicki ran after Judd through the pouring rain. They hit the edge of the woods, and both went tumbling into the wet leaves and mud. Lightning flashed, and Vicki saw they were on the edge of a drop-off.

"They'll think we're headed for the drain-pipe," Judd yelled. "We have to find a place to hide."

Vicki's heart pounded. She had been upset with Judd for being so bossy. Now she didn't mind. "How about up there?" she said, pointing to a gnarled pile of wood and leaves.

"Good," Judd said. "We can get out as soon as we see them go toward the drain."

Vicki and Judd scampered back up the hillside and covered themselves with wet leaves. The rain pelted them. Vicki was glad to see the dogs enter the woods fifty yards from them. Judd and Vicki lay perfectly still. Lightning flashed again.

When it was clear the men were going toward the drain, Judd whispered, "If they see us, don't stop. Keep running for the cave as fast as you can."

Vicki nodded. Judd ran through the trees ahead of her. She didn't dare look back.

Lionel plugged in the laptop when he reached the computer room. The battery would need an hour or two to recharge. Rummaging through the scattered contents of the desk, he was surprised to find two batteries. He put them next to the laptop and ran to the hangar.

Lionel found the supplies but left them there. Something bothered him. If the GC came back and found his wet tracks leading to the hideout, he was sunk. While the GC were looking for Judd and Vicki there was time.

Lionel looked for some rags and found a

stack of blankets near the food stash. He took off his shoes and socks, still dripping from the rain, and climbed through the opening. On his hands and knees, he dried the wet spots. Something in the entryway caught his eye. It had a greenish glow. He inched his way over on top of the blanket.

On the floor next to one of the chairs was a cell phone. The display glowed with the last number the man had dialed.

Suddenly the room lit up with the searchlight of the passing helicopter. Lionel scrambled into the shadows. He stuck the phone in his pocket and crawled toward the hideout.

Back in the computer room he inspected the phone closely. He found the ringer and turned it off. He looked through the list of numbers. One of them said *Comm. B.*

Lionel clipped the phone to his belt and moved to the hangar. He spread three blankets on the floor. In the first he loaded bottles of water. In the second and third he placed the dried and canned food. He tied each blanket and lugged all three to the landing near the picture. He would be ready when the kids returned the following night.

With the physical work complete, Lionel sat at the computer. The battery was 50 percent charged. He pulled out Judd's instructions and opened Conrad's message.

Don't reply to this, Conrad wrote. *Wherever you are, stay there. The GC are still looking, but don't have a clue. I'm trying to get Darrion out, but it might take some time. I'll be in touch as soon as I can. Conrad.*

Lionel smiled and deleted the message.

Conrad got out of the jeep first. "I'm gonna get some sleep."

"Give us the disk," Melinda said.

"No problem," Conrad said. He pulled the disk from his pocket and gave it to Felicia.

"It's broken!" Felicia said.

Conrad grabbed the disk and shook his head. "It must have cracked when I jumped on the guy," he said.

Conrad went toward his room, then ducked behind a building. Melinda and Felicia turned and headed toward the commander's tent.

When they hit the clearing, Judd looked toward the Stahley house. A helicopter hovered with its searchlight trained on the mansion. He hoped Lionel hadn't been caught.

"Keep going," Judd said as he and Vicki stayed close to the ground. The rain came down at an angle, stinging Judd's face.

Judd couldn't find the opening or Mark's signal. The dogs bellowed from inside the drainpipe. Vicki tripped over something in the grass.

Mark stuck his head out of the hole. "Thought you guys were goners," he said. "Get in here."

Judd and Vicki crawled onto the ledge with Mark. Shelly made room for them and started down the rope.

"Flashlight's batteries are almost out," Mark said. "I stopped signaling you a while ago."

Before the hatch closed, a flash of lightning lit up the cave. Judd squinted at the floor. He grabbed the light from Mark and turned it on.

"You're gonna run it totally—"

"Shelly, stop!" Judd screamed. "Stay right where you are."

"I can't hang on," Shelly said.

"What is it?" Vicki said.

The dim light barely showed the horror of what lay a few feet beneath Shelly.

"Snakes," Judd said. "The cave floor is full of them!"

Lionel found a message from Mr. Stein. He opened it and read the information about Conrad.

They were just here, Mr. Stein wrote. *Conrad left a message. Please write as soon as possible. I have wonderful news.*

Lionel pulled out the phone and dialed the number Mr. Stein included at the bottom of his E-mail.

"How did you get a phone?" Mr. Stein said.

"Long story," Lionel said. "Are you sure this line isn't tapped?"

"I don't believe it is."

"Good," Lionel said. "What's the news?"

"My daughter's prayers have been answered," Mr. Stein said. "I have become a believer in Jesus Christ."

Lionel nearly dropped the phone. "That's great," he said.

"I have been reading Dr. Ben-Judah's Web site," Mr. Stein continued. "I tried to contact him."

"Judging from the amount of mail he's getting, that's a long shot," Lionel said.

"I believe God has chosen me to be one of his witnesses," Mr. Stein said. "I want to go to Israel and attend the meeting. It is only a few weeks away."

"Sir, we're in deep trouble here," Lionel said.

"Of course," Mr. Stein said. "How can I help?"

"The message you received from Conrad," Lionel said. "Read it to me." When Mr. Stein finished, Lionel said, "I don't know about letting Darrion go much longer with the commander."

"It sounds as if Conrad has the situation under control," Mr. Stein said. He described the threat on his life by Felicia and Melinda. "If Conrad can get the GC to trust him, he'll have a better chance to get her out. But, as he says here, it may take up to two weeks."

"What about Israel?" Lionel said.

"You are my friends," Mr. Stein said. "I'm sure God will work something out."

"If the GC get your phone records, they'll find out about this call. It won't look good."

"I'm willing to risk anything," Mr. Stein said. "Tell me where you are. I will come get you."

"No," Lionel said. "We've found a safe place."

"Once Conrad sets the plan in motion, do

you have anyone to help you surprise the GC while you get away?"

"I'll talk with Judd," Lionel said.

Lionel heard movement above him and whispered, "I'll call you tomorrow night." He turned off the phone and listened as the GC entered the house.

"Don't look down!" Judd shouted to Shelly as she swayed above the cave floor.

"I can't hang on much longer," Shelly said.

"The water must have made them go for higher ground," Mark said.

"Are they poisonous?" Vicki said.

"I don't want to take the chance," Judd said, grabbing the rope and climbing down as quickly as he could. He didn't want to knock Shelly off, but he knew she wouldn't be able to climb up by herself.

Mark held the flashlight. Judd saw Vicki cover her eyes.

"I don't feel well," Shelly said.

"Hang in there, Shel," Judd said. "You've gotta help me climb back to the top."

When Judd got near, he let go with his legs and slid close to Shelly. "Put your arms around me and hold tight," he said.

Shelly grabbed Judd's belt with one hand

and tried to pull herself up. She slipped, but Judd caught her with a hand. Shelly put her arms around Judd's neck.

Judd hung on while Mark and Vicki pulled the rope up an inch at a time. When they made it to the ledge, Judd collapsed. Shelly fell into Vicki's arms, crying.

"Maybe we should have made a run for it," Mark said.

Judd tried to catch his breath. The rain was coming harder, and the chopper wasn't going away.

SEVEN

Night Moves

JUDD was drained. The kids couldn't go through another night like this. But Lionel needed them. *What if Lionel was caught?* Judd pushed the thought from his mind.

Shelly, Vicki, and Mark braced themselves at the top of the cave. Judd knew they couldn't stay in that position all night.

"My leg's cramping," Vicki said.

Judd turned on the dim flashlight and scanned the floor. The cave was dry. The snakes weren't leaving. Judd noticed an area under them that the snakes avoided.

"I'm not going down there," Shelly said.

"If you go to sleep, you'll fall," Judd said.

"I'm not going down," Shelly said.

Judd climbed down the rope. He didn't know much about snakes, but he could tell many of them weren't poisonous. He knew that wouldn't make the others feel much better.

Judd noticed a ledge to his left. The rock wasn't wet and there were no snakes. He threw a rock, which hit with a thud. The snakes hissed and moved back. Judd described the ledge, but Vicki and Shelly shook their heads.

"There's room for all of us to stretch out and sleep," Judd said. "We're going to need the rest."

"We need food," Shelly said.

"We'll get it tomorrow when Lionel gets back," Judd said.

"Why don't we sleep in the meadow tonight?" Vicki said.

The helicopter passed again, slivers of light shining through cracks in the opening above them.

"Any more questions?" Judd said.

"So if we go down there, what's to keep our squirmy little friends off us?" Mark said.

"I'll take the first watch," Judd said. "They're just as afraid of us as we are of them."

"Right," Shelly said. "They don't look scared to me."

Judd led the way down and helped Vicki, Shelly, and Mark onto the ledge. The girls were wary of the snakes, but Judd assured them he would keep watch.

Judd turned the flashlight on every minute or so. He threw rocks and sand at the snakes that came near.

A few minutes later, Judd heard the soft breathing of the others as they slept. Judd stretched his legs and yawned. The rainfall overhead and the occasional clap of thunder brought back memories. When a storm would come in the night, he would run into his parents' room and sleep by their bed.

He threw a few more rocks toward the snakes and stretched out by the ledge. The flashlight was almost useless now. With its dim light he could see only a few feet away.

Judd felt his eyes getting heavier. He shook himself awake. He had to stay awake.

Lionel heard the Global Community guards return. The helicopter widened its search and finally gave up. The GC radios squawked upstairs, but Lionel couldn't make out the conversation from his hideout.

Lionel finished preparing the supplies and checked the computer. He pulled out a blanket and curled up in the computer room. He knew he would need the rest for the night ahead.

He awoke refreshed a few hours later and

plugged in another battery. He turned the computer speakers off and logged on to Judd's E-mail. A message from Dr. Ben-Judah caught his eye.

Judd, I know you have been concerned about Chloe, and our prayers have been answered. Buck has returned with her. She has many injuries from the earthquake, but if she hadn't run from her home, she would have died. Thank God she and the baby are all right.

"The baby?" Lionel said out loud. He smiled. So Buck and Chloe were going to have a baby. Cool. Lionel wanted to see Vicki's face when she found out.

Buck is nervous about my plans to travel to Israel, Tsion continued, *but I know this is of God. I will go there if it is his will.*

Please pray for this and another matter. Buck and Chloe have a friend who is in terrible trouble. I won't go into the details, but this woman needs God in her life.

Let me know how I can help. I pray for you daily.

Tsion closed with a verse of encouragement. Lionel put his head on the desk. It had been so long since he had experienced a normal day. He longed to sit in a church service with other believers, or in a small group and talk about the Bible. Lionel couldn't imagine when that would happen, or if it would ever happen again.

Vicki awoke stiff and cold. She noticed a bit of morning light coming through the top of the cave. The rain had stopped. She looked at Judd and gasped. He was asleep, and several snakes were lying next to him.

Something heavy was on her legs. She lifted her head. Two huge snakes stretched out beside her. Another had crawled on top of her legs.

Vicki trembled and tried not to scream. She looked at Shelly and Mark. The snakes hadn't gotten to them.

"Help," she whispered. She said it three more times before Mark awoke.

"OK," Mark said, wiping the sleep from his eyes. "They've just found a warm place. Don't make any sudden movements."

"Get them off me," Vicki said.

Mark looked behind him and grabbed a long stick. "Lie back and don't watch," he said.

Vicki closed her eyes. Mark lifted the snake with the stick. Vicki opened her eyes and saw the snake's head inches from her face. Mark threw the snake to the other side of the cave and it landed with a thud. He pushed the two other snakes away from Vicki, and she scooted closer to Shelly.

Mark climbed off the ledge and put his hand over Judd's mouth. He whispered something to him. Mark picked the snakes off one by one and threw them in the corner. Shelly watched in horror. When the snakes were gone, Judd stood and leaned against the ledge.

Judd shook his head. "I'm sorry," he said. "Couldn't keep my eyes open."

Shelly stood and said, "I'm not staying here another night."

"We have to get Lionel out," Judd said.

"I don't care if I get caught by the GC," Shelly said. "I don't care if they throw me in jail or put me in a reeducation camp. Anything's better than living like this."

"Look!" Mark said, pointing to the other side of the cave.

Vicki squinted and noticed the room full of snakes had disappeared. Only the ones Mark had thrown on the other side remained.

"We have to keep our heads," Judd said.

Shelly jumped down, watching each step closely. "I'm telling you, I'm climbing out of here now."

Judd nodded to Mark. Mark grabbed Shelly and held her by the arm.

"If you don't let go, I'll scream!"

"If you climb out of here now, it could endanger the rest of us," Judd said.

Shelly cried. "You don't understand."

Vicki climbed from the ledge and put an arm around Shelly. The girl was falling apart. Vicki didn't want to stay in the cave any more than Shelly did, but Judd was right.

Vicki tried to calm her, but Shelly began to shake and sob. "I have to get out!" she screamed.

Vicki put an arm around Shelly. "What's going on?" she said.

It took Shelly a few minutes to calm down. "I feel so bad," she cried. "I'm trying to hold together, but I can't."

"It's OK that you lost it," Vicki said. "I'm scared of the snakes, too."

"Not like me," Shelly said. "When I was little, my mom left me and went to a bar. I was playing in the backyard. We had a rusty, old slide and a swing. There was this snake sunning itself on the end, but I didn't see it."

"How awful," Vicki said.

"I tried to stop, but I couldn't. I knocked it onto the ground. It probably wasn't poisonous, but it scared me. I cried and cried, but my mom was out drinking. Every time I see snakes, it comes back to me. I'm so sorry."

Shelly put her head on Vicki's shoulder. "It's OK," Vicki said.

After a fitful night's sleep, Conrad reported to the commander's office with Melinda and Felicia. The commander had circles under his eyes, and his jaw was tight.

"The Stahley girl still hasn't talked," the commander said. "Without food or water she should be starving by now."

Conrad knew why Darrion hadn't starved. In addition to the candy bar, he had gotten two bottles of water and some sandwiches to her.

"We're putting a ring around the Stahley place," the commander continued. "There must be something inside that house the kids want."

"Sir, could we have another go at her?" Melinda said.

The commander nodded and looked at his computer. The screen saver was a flying insignia of the Global Community that morphed into the smiling face of Nicolae Carpathia.

"The top brass is asking questions," the commander said. "They've heard there's been trouble. I've been able to cover so far, but they want to know if we can supply Morale Monitors in the new schools."

"When will they need them?" Conrad said.

"Next month," the commander said.

Melinda stood. "Give us another chance," she said. "We'll get something out of her."

While he was on-line, Lionel saw a window pop up. It was Pavel, Judd's friend from New Babylon. Lionel turned on the speakers and looked at the boy.

"You are not Judd," Pavel said.

"I'm his friend Lionel."

"Your face is in shadows," Pavel said. "Lean closer to the camera so I can see your forehead."

When Lionel did, the boy smiled. "It is good to talk with you, my brother," Pavel said. "Where is Judd?"

Lionel explained their situation. Pavel gasped. "I was afraid things would get worse for Judd."

"What's going on over there?" Lionel said.

"Nicolae Carpathia is angered by the response to Tsion Ben-Judah's Web site," Pavel said. "It is being read by millions around the world. The potentate himself has been reading it."

"What for?" Lionel said.

"My father says the Global Community wants to sponsor the rabbi's return to Israel. It's supposed to show how loving the potentate is. I believe he has sinister plans."

"The rabbi's smart," Lionel said. "He won't walk into an ambush. Besides, the GC should look at what Tsion is saying about the one-world faith."

"That is another interesting story," Pavel said. "The potentate is at odds with Enigma Babylon's top man."

"You mean Mathews?"

"Correct. Mathews thinks he and the one-world religion are bigger than the Global Community."

"So Carpathia has competition and he doesn't like it," Lionel said.

"He doesn't like Mathews or Ben-Judah, and he hates the preachers at the Wailing Wall. He's convinced they're speaking to him."

"Wouldn't be surprised if they are," Lionel said.

"My father heard him scream, 'I want them dead! And soon!'"

Lionel shook his head. It had been a long time since he had seen the prophets Moishe and Eli. They would tell the truth about Nicolae and wouldn't hold back. Lionel couldn't wait to tell the others what he had learned.

"One more thing," Pavel said. "My father had a talk with a man in Carpathia's communications department yesterday. He told him there are missiles pointing into outer space."

"Missiles?" Lionel said.

"The potentate is afraid of meteors sent by God."

Conrad winced when Melinda slapped Darrion across the face. Darrion didn't answer her questions. She only looked at the girls and said, "Water. I need water."

Felicia took her turn hitting Darrion and yelling at her. Conrad knew they expected the same from him.

He kicked Darrion's chair out from under her and shoved her under the table. Out of sight he winked. "You're doing great," he whispered. "Keep it up."

Judd knew if anyone could calm Shelly, it was Vicki. Shelly kept saying she had to get out. Judd and Mark stayed back.

"She's losing it," Mark whispered.

"I can't blame her," Judd said. "I should have stayed awake."

"We'll get Lionel back in a few hours," Mark said. "A fire and some food will change things."

Judd nodded. He wanted to believe Mark was right, but he wasn't sure.

Lionel heard more movement upstairs and crept near the GC officers. One was talking on the radio.

"Go ahead, Commander," the man said.

Lionel felt a chill when he heard his boss's voice.

"Ferguson, you and Wilcox stay there until nightfall," the commander said. "We'll send a chopper for you."

"What if they come back, sir?" the man said.

"I think they've moved on," the commander said. "No use wasting manpower."

When the commander was through, Ferguson said to Wilcox, "Awful lot of trouble to go through for a bunch of kids."

"He wants to make a lesson of this one," Wilcox said as he rattled a piece of paper. "Washington. Kid made him look bad."

"He's not gonna exactly throw a party for the other two, Byrne and Thompson."

"Cute girl," Wilcox said. "Wonder what they did?"

"Get your stuff together," Ferguson said. "We'll catch 'em. And when we do, the commander will make sure none of these little Morale Monitors ever cross him again."

EIGHT

Lionel's Discovery

THE commander's conversation had left Lionel uneasy. He should have been happy the GC were pulling out. That would make things easier. They wouldn't have to stay in the cave. But the way the commander talked troubled Lionel. Something didn't seem right.

Lionel took the three packs of provisions and put the most important stuff into one blanket. Food, water, matches, and the laptop. All the batteries were charged, so the kids would have enough power for hours of computer use.

Lionel dug his way through the mound of dirt that covered the secret entrance. When he was nearly through, he pulled out the GC officer's phone and scrolled through the list of names and landed on *Comm. B.* Lionel punched the Send button and listened.

"Ferguson?" an aide to the commander said.

"Yeah," Lionel said, trying to sound like Ferguson.

"Glad you called. Commander wanted me to give you a message. You found your cell phone?"

"Yeah, it was under the chair," Lionel said.

"Too bad," the aide said.

"What do you mean?"

"You know, we hoped whoever was in the house had taken it."

"Right," Lionel said. *They know I'm in the house!*

"Here's the plan," the aide said. "You and Wilcox make a big deal about getting out of there. Slam the door, whatever you have to do. Flank the house on both sides until your backup comes. They'll be there within the hour."

"How many are you sending?" Lionel said.

"We went over this," the aide barked. "We'll have a chopper and ten men. Now the kids may try to come back in, or the one inside will go to the others. It's important we get them all."

"I got it," Lionel said. He hung up the phone and gave a low whistle. He only had one chance, and he had to act fast.

Vicki stayed with Shelly the whole day. Staying at the top of the cave had calmed Shelly. Vicki left her only once to get her a drink of water, but Judd stopped her.

"This stuff needs to be boiled before we drink it," Judd said.

"She needs something," Vicki pleaded. "Let me just give her a little."

"It'll make her sick," Judd said.

Vicki stomped off and climbed the rope again. She put her feet on the side of the cave to balance herself. The more she did it, the better she got at climbing.

"Just a few more hours," Vicki said. "We'll get a fire going, get some food and water—"

"I don't have the strength to help tonight," Shelly said.

"It's OK," Vicki said. "You rest, and we'll take care of getting Lionel."

Vicki watched Mark and Judd gather the remaining sticks and wood from the cave. She was so hungry. Her mouth was dry and her lips cracked. The only good news was that the snakes were gone. But Vicki wondered if they would return if it started raining again.

Lionel shoved the blanket filled with provisions through the hole until it almost fell out the other side. He didn't hear a chopper or any GC troops. He crawled on hands and knees to the middle of the opening and pulled the cell phone from his pocket. He found the number listed for Larry Wilcox and pushed Send.

The guard with the deep voice answered. "Wilcox."

"Ferguson still hasn't found his phone?" Lionel said angrily.

"No, sir," Wilcox said. "We think—"

"Never mind what you think," Lionel interrupted. "The commander wants you inside until the chopper gets there with the others."

"All right," Wilcox said.

"Where are the dogs?" Lionel said.

"Outside, on either side of the house, like we were told," Wilcox said.

"Bring them in," Lionel said.

"But, sir—"

"Do you want me to get the commander on the line?" Lionel said.

"No, sir," Wilcox said. "We'll bring them in right away."

Lionel waited a few minutes, then pushed

the pack of provisions the rest of the way out with his feet. He wiped the dirt from his face and looked around. Light was fading. No one was in sight. He grabbed the heavy pack, slung it onto his back, and took off for the meadow.

He heard a faint rumbling in the distance. On the horizon he spotted a helicopter. It was still at least a mile away. Lionel ran as fast as he could toward the cave.

Judd went over the plan once again. He and Mark would go for Lionel while Vicki and Shelly stayed behind. Vicki seemed miffed that she didn't get to go, but Judd wasn't going to worry about that now.

"Somebody's coming!" Shelly said from the top of the cave.

"Quick," Judd said, "get down!"

Judd pulled out his gun and aimed it at the opening. Dirt fell as someone tried to get in.

"Lionel!" Vicki shouted.

"Somebody give me a hand with this stuff," Lionel said as he replaced the door. Judd climbed up to help. Shelly and Vicki tore into the blanket and found the water.

"Why didn't you wait for us?" Judd said.

Lionel told him what he'd discovered. In the middle of his story he stopped. "Chopper's landing," he said. "If I'd have stayed, they'd have caught you guys for sure."

Judd lit a match, but Lionel blew it out. "The GC might see the smoke," he said.

The five ate and drank until they were full. Lionel spread the supplies out and showed them the phone and laptop. "We'll have to conserve the food," he said.

"How long are we gonna be here?" Shelly said.

"The GC won't give up looking for us," Lionel said. "I think we have to wait here until we find a better place."

"No way," Shelly said.

"What about Conrad and Darrion?" Vicki said.

"Conrad's message said for us to stay where we are," Lionel said. "Until we run out of supplies, I think that's exactly what we should do."

"Anything has to be better than this," Shelly said. She told Lionel about the snakes.

"I don't like snakes any more than you," Lionel said, "but—"

"I'm telling you, I can't stand another night in here," Shelly said.

Lionel nodded. "I know you're scared, but there are a dozen GC troops out there right now looking for us. If they find one of us, they'll find the rest. You might get off with a reeducation camp. But they'll court-martial me, and who knows what they'll do to Judd and Vicki."

Shelly looked away.

"We'll keep you safe," Judd said.

Shelly stood. "That's what you said last night. I just can't handle another night in here, OK?"

Shelly walked away.

Lionel told the others about his conversations with Pavel and Mr. Stein. When Vicki heard the news about Mr. Stein and his belief in Christ, tears welled up in her eyes. "I wish Chaya were here," she said.

"There's something else," Lionel said. "Chloe's going to have a baby."

Vicki's mouth dropped open and she cried harder.

Judd grabbed the cell phone. Lionel showed him the number. Mr. Stein answered.

"Are you all right?" Mr. Stein said. "I was so worried after talking with Lionel this morning."

"We're OK," Judd said. "Lionel told us about you."

Mr. Stein chuckled. "Do you know that I am probably one of the 144,000 witnesses?"

"I imagine so," Judd said.

"There is so much to learn. I need to meet with you and Vicki. I want to become strong and tell others about God. Just like the apostle Paul."

"Keep reading Tsion's Web site," Judd said.

"I am. But I've also written Nicolae Carpathia."

"You what?" Judd said.

"There were so many messages pleading with the potentate to provide safety for the rabbi. I wrote Nicolae himself and said surely a lover of peace, who helped the rabbi escape his homeland, has the power to return him safely to Israel."

"Carpathia took the credit for getting Ben-Judah out of Israel?" Judd said. "Buck said—"

"Of course he took credit," Mr. Stein said. "He wanted to look good in the eyes of the world."

"Did you get a reply?"

"Not with words," Mr. Stein said. "This afternoon, Global Community officers appeared and took my computer away. I have others, of course. They asked again about my involvement with Vicki."

"What did you say?" Judd said.

"I told them the truth. I don't know where she is."

Judd heard a click on the line.

"I have withdrawn all my money from—"

"Mr. Stein," Judd said, "hang up and get to a safe place."

"What's wrong?"

"I think someone's listening."

"But Dr. Ben-Judah believes each of the witnesses is protected by God. Not everyone who has the mark on their forehead is protected. Only the 144,000 evangelists."

"Then be safe and get out of there."

"All right," Mr. Stein said. "But how will I reach you?"

"Use my E-mail address and tell me where to call you," Judd said. "Hurry."

Lionel and the others prayed that Mr. Stein would get to a safe place. Though their gathering wasn't the church setting Lionel had longed for, just being with other believers made him feel better. He prayed for Shelly and asked that her fear of the cave be taken away.

When they were through, Lionel hooked up the laptop. Just like the food, they would need to ration the use of the computer.

"If the batteries last as long as they say," Lionel said, "we could go forty minutes a day for more than three weeks."

"You think we could be in here that long?" Vicki said.

"I think we have to prepare for the worst," Lionel said.

Lionel logged on to the site where Eli and Moishe were shown live each day. The camera at the Wailing Wall carried live audio as well. Lionel knew these were the two preachers predicted in the book of Revelation. Judd pointed out their smoky burlap robes. They wore no shoes and had dark, bony feet and knuckled hands.

"They look like they're a thousand years old," Vicki said.

Their beards and hair were long, and they had dark, piercing eyes. They screamed out warnings to those who continued to reject Jesus as Messiah. As some in the crowd protested, Eli said, "Do not mock the Holy One of Israel! He came that you might have life, and have it to the full."

"Woe to you who reject the Son of God," he said. The camera showed a close-up of Eli's face. It was leathery and sunbaked. "And woe to those who fall prey to the one who sits on the throne of this earth."

"Who's he talking about?" Vicki said.

"The only person I can think of is Nicolae Carpathia," Lionel said.

Conrad rushed to the commander's tent with Melinda and Felicia. The commander smiled and came out to meet them.

"We've just heard a conversation between Stein and Thompson," the commander said. "This guy fooled us. He is in contact with them, and he's one of the fanatics. Told Thompson he was part of their elite group of 144,000, whatever that means."

The commander answered a phone call. When he was finished, he slammed the phone to the ground.

"The computer they took from his home came up empty," the commander said. "But we have enough on him now."

"What will you do, sir?" Conrad said.

"Question him and see if he'll talk now that we have him on tape," the commander said. "If he doesn't tell us what we want, we'll execute him."

"And if he does tell you?" Conrad said.

The commander smiled. "We'll execute him anyway."

NINE

The Plan

FOR the next three weeks, Judd tried to make contact with his friend Pete. Pete had access to motorcycles, but he hadn't returned Judd's calls. The kids all agreed they would be safer away from the Mount Prospect area, but none of them wanted to leave without Conrad or Darrion.

Judd and the others coaxed Shelly into staying. She slept in the highest spot in the cave each night and kept an eye out for snakes. Vicki still talked about finding Phoenix. Judd tried not to discourage her, but he didn't hold out much hope.

"Maybe that biker group got Pete," Vicki said. "After what happened at that gas station, they sounded pretty upset."

"That's it," Judd said. He phoned the gas station and left a message.

Their food was running low, but Judd

knew if they were careful, they could last a few more days. Judd and Mark had made two midnight attempts to retrieve more supplies. Each time, they had to turn back. The GC still had guards posted at the house.

Though there was enough room in the cave, the kids quickly got restless. Each time they accessed the Internet, Mark searched for his cousin John. After two weeks he still had no word.

Judd and the others limited their computer time to twenty minutes each morning and twenty minutes each night. It was their only contact with the outside world.

One evening they gathered around the computer, and Judd read aloud an E-mail from Tsion Ben-Judah.

If you see media reports about a shooting in Denver, it is true that Buck was there, Tsion wrote. *Don't believe anything else about the reports.*

Judd clicked on a news flash and saw a video of the shooting in Colorado. The reporter said, "Two men, one claiming to be Nicolae Carpathia's pilot, broke into this clinic and killed a receptionist and a guard."

Footage from security cameras showed blurry video footage of three men.

"Isn't that Buck in the middle?" Vicki said.

Judd nodded. "Tsion said something about a friend of Chloe's being in trouble," he said.

The video showed a picture of a woman embracing Nicolae Carpathia. "That's Hattie Durham!" Vicki said.

"The two killers reportedly abducted the fiancée of Potentate Nicolae Carpathia," the reporter said. "The public is asked to provide any information about the identities of these men, or the whereabouts of Ms. Hattie Durham."

The news channel showed an enhanced photo of Buck and another man, along with Hattie Durham. Judd shook his head. "I want to hear Buck's version of what happened," he said.

With their water running low and no word from Pete, Judd had to make a decision. They hadn't heard from Mr. Stein, and Judd feared the man had been caught. His fears were confirmed the next morning when Conrad sent an urgent message.

We brought Mr. Stein in late last night, Conrad wrote. *He stayed hidden as long as he could, but we got a call from one of the shelters. He went for food, and someone recognized him from a photo the GC had passed around.*

I was with Melinda and Felicia when we found him. He's lost a lot of weight. He saw me and almost said something. I felt so bad taking him in. The commander's questioning him now. He's threatening to execute him if he doesn't give you guys up. Behind closed doors the commander says he'll execute him by noon, no matter what.

"That's in a few hours!" Vicki said.

Judd kept reading the message. *I don't know what to do. The commander is talking about shipping Darrion away by the end of the week. If we're going to do anything, now's the time.*

Judd turned off the computer and hung his head. "We're going to get him out of there," he said. "Darrion too."

"How?" Mark said.

Judd's phone rang.

"Hey, pal, what's up?" Pete said.

Judd told Pete their situation.

"I want to help," Pete said, "but there's no way I can make it by noon. Need time to get other riders together."

"What about tomorrow?" Judd said. "If we can stall them long enough, we have a chance of getting our people out."

"Sounds good," Pete said. "I can meet you at eight tonight, then have my other people there in the morning."

Judd gave Pete directions and thanked him.

"Hey, you saved my life," Pete said. "Plus, I've been wanting to see you. I have a surprise."

Every day Conrad felt more confident about his standing with Commander Blancka, Melinda, and Felicia. The girls no longer whispered when he was around. Together, Conrad and the girls followed leads and looked for Lionel and the others.

Commander Blancka was astounded that Darrion could last so long without food or water. Conrad knew he was taking a great risk slipping Darrion her provisions. He had now come up with a different plan. During one of their meetings he spied a letter in Commander Blancka's trash sent by an upper-level GC officer. He stuffed it in his pocket while no one was looking, then photocopied the insignia onto another sheet. He wrote a brief note that said, *A starving girl in a GC prison would not reflect well on the potentate or his friends.*

Conrad found a plain brown envelope and scribbled *T. B.*, the commander's initials, on the outside. When Melinda and Felicia were on an assignment, Conrad rushed to the commander's tent.

"I was told to give this to you, sir," Conrad said.

Conrad turned to leave as the commander opened the envelope.

"Hold on," the commander said. "Who gave you this?"

"I'm not sure, sir," Conrad said. "I've never seen him before. He headed back toward the airfield."

"Did you read this?"

"Should I have, sir?" Conrad said.

The commander scratched his chin. "No, I just wish I knew who was behind it."

The next day Darrion received three meals.

Conrad had very little contact with Darrion after that. Only a wink or a nod in the interview room when no one was looking. Conrad listened closely and tried to pick up information.

A chill ran through Conrad as he heard the commander talk about Mr. Stein. "After tomorrow there'll be one less fanatic in the world," the commander said.

Judd talked over the plan with the others, and they agreed it was their best shot to save Mr. Stein's life. Judd dialed the number. Commander Blancka's aide answered gruffly.

"This is Judd Thompson. I want to speak with the commander."

Conrad watched as the aide rushed in and handed the commander the phone. "It's Thompson," the aide said.

"Are Washington and Byrne with you?" the commander said.

Conrad's plan to save Mr. Stein was to try and whisk the man from the back of the jail. But Conrad knew that would endanger his rescue of Darrion, who was now being held in a different area.

"What do you propose?" the commander said.

"First of all, if you harm Mr. Stein in any way, or if the girl is harmed, the deal's off."

"You're making a deal with *me?*" the commander said. "You're not in that kind of position."

"I'm one of three people you want in custody," Judd said. "From the way you guarded that house, you want us bad."

"And I'm still going to get you."

"I'm offering an even trade," Judd said. "I'll come in if you let them go."

The commander laughed. "No deal. I want Washington and that Byrne girl too."

"Three for two?" Judd said. "Doesn't sound fair to me."

The commander lowered his voice. "Thompson, I can make it easy for you. Are the other two right there?"

"I can talk."

"We have to make you pay for what you did to GC property," the commander said. "Honestly, you'll be in and out in a couple months max. I'll put in a good word for you."

"I thought you were the one making the decisions," Judd said. "If I need to talk with someone else—"

"You're right," the commander interrupted. "I do make the decisions, but those are always reviewed. Now, I'm willing to work with you, and I assume that by your call you're willing to work with me."

"What about Vicki and Lionel?"

"Now's not the time to concern yourself with them. Byrne has a murder rap and an escape on her head. Washington . . . we have to make an example of him. But I'll do what I can. You just come in—"

"You have to assure me that Mr. Stein and Darrion won't be hurt," Judd said.

"We can hold off on our plans for him if you come in today," the commander said.

"Tomorrow," Judd said. "Five o'clock at New Hope Village Church."

Judd hung up.

Conrad studied the commander's face as he told them what Judd had said.

"Couldn't we trace the call?" Melinda said.

"Not with a GC phone," the commander said. "Unfortunately, they have one."

"What are you going to do?" Felicia said.

"We're going to give them the girl and Stein," the commander said. Conrad began to protest. The commander held up a hand. "They're going to walk into a trap, and you three are going to be there to watch it."

Judd volunteered to meet Pete at the bridge. The others had questions about how they were going to overpower the commander and get away.

"You know they'll be waiting for us," Mark said.

"That's where Conrad comes in," Judd said. "He'll be working from the inside."

Vicki shook her head. "If Mr. Stein is right and he's one of the 144,000 witnesses, he's going to come through this. But we don't have that kind of guarantee."

"You're not actually planning on having us all there, are you?" Shelly said.

"That's the plan right now," Judd said. "We'll talk with Pete—"

"I don't need to talk with anybody," Shelly said. "You've kept me cooped up here for weeks and for what? You want me to surrender to this commander guy? No way."

Judd held up a hand. "We want to get Darrion and Mr. Stein out of the GC hands, right? If somebody has a better plan than this, I'm open to it. Let me go get Pete, and we'll see how he can help us."

Judd plastered mud on his face and tunneled through the wall of mud and rocks in the drainpipe. He listened carefully when he came to the mouth of the pipe and didn't hear anything.

The sky was cloudy and made traveling difficult. He didn't want to use Lionel's flashlight until he had to. It had been weeks since Judd was outside. The smell of the earth and the fresh air made Judd feel alive.

He climbed over fallen trees and up steep hillsides along the riverbank. Judd saw the lights of the bridge in the distance. He moved cautiously toward it.

The bridge was complete, though it looked

nothing like it once did. Pieces of plywood covered the holes. At the other side sat two GC guards.

Judd crawled beneath the bridge and waited. With his back against a pylon, he nearly fell asleep. In the distance he heard a rumbling and saw two headlights approach.

The guards looked over some papers and waved the two ahead. When the cycles neared the end, Judd signaled the lead driver with Lionel's flashlight.

Pete parked his cycle and ran down the embankment toward Judd. The two embraced. Judd had to catch his breath after Pete's hug. He was as big and burly as ever.

"Good to see you," Pete whispered. "Been praying for you."

"We've got a big job ahead of us tomorrow," Judd said. "I'm not sure we're up to it."

"God is," Pete said. "I've seen him do some amazing things the past few weeks."

The other rider parked his motorcycle and walked with a limp toward Judd and Pete. He was tall and thin.

"I almost forgot," Pete said. "You're gonna love this."

Judd stared at the man. Bruises and scratches covered his face.

"Don't you recognize him?" Pete said.

Judd fell back against the bridge and gasped. "It can't be," he said.

TEN

Taylor's Story

JUDD blinked. "Is it really you?" he said.

Taylor Graham dropped his helmet and goggles and put out his hand. Judd noticed a huge bruise on the side of his head.

"Didn't think you'd ever see me again, huh?" Taylor said.

"I saw you go over the cliff," Judd said. "I looked for your body."

"The log hit me in the head," Taylor said. "I stayed conscious until I went over. When I woke up, I was on a ledge next to the water. Bodies were floating everywhere."

"I hate to break up this reunion," Pete said, "but those guards are gonna get suspicious."

Judd helped Pete and Taylor hide their motorcycles under the bridge. The three ran toward the meadow. Taylor asked about the

Stahley hangar, and Judd briefly told him their story.

"How's Ryan?" Taylor said.

Judd took a deep breath and told him about Ryan's death.

Taylor shook his head. "He was a good kid," he said.

The three slipped through the top of the cave. Judd introduced Pete and Taylor to the others.

"Finish your story," Judd said. "How'd you get out of that lake and hook up with Pete?"

"Hank and Judy," Taylor said. "I couldn't climb out myself, so I just waited to die. I don't know how long it was, but this farmer and his wife spotted me and got a rope long enough to reach."

"The same couple who helped me," Judd said.

"After I told them about the quake and the van, they said you had been there and left. I wasn't in any shape to travel, so they let me have their son's room."

Judd explained that the couple were also tribulation saints and had a son who had died in the earthquake.

"A couple of days later GC guards came by," Taylor continued. "A few people from the reeducation camp had escaped. Hank and Judy covered for me. They told me their story. Tried to get me to believe like them."

Judd looked closely at Taylor's forehead. There was no mark. "They're really good people," Judd said.

"They *were* good people," Pete said. "I went to see 'em a few days after I met this guy. The GC had come back and found out they'd been hiding people."

"What happened to them?" Vicki said.

"They were executed on the spot," Pete said.

Vicki gasped.

"This guy almost got himself killed too," Taylor said, pointing to Pete.

Pete shook his head. "Wasn't like that," he said. "I was just giving some friends the gospel."

"Your former biker group?" Judd said.

"We had a score to settle at that gas station," Pete said. "I found the owner and told him about Jesus. Said he wasn't into religion, but he was impressed with the way I'd helped a stranger. So he prayed with me like I did with you.

"Next thing I know, the gang is back. That's when Taylor comes walking into the middle of our fight. Only it turns out not to be a fight."

Taylor laughed. "This big monster was preaching to the rest of them. Couldn't believe it."

"It was the second time I'd told them," Pete said. "Not everybody responded the way I wanted, but most of them believed. They're coming to help tomorrow."

Lionel listened to the stories and held back as long as he could. He could see the resemblance of Conrad in Taylor's face.

When there was a lull, Lionel said, "I know your brother. He's been worried about you."

"Conrad?" Taylor said. "How do you know him?"

Lionel explained how the two had met. "Conrad's working on the inside trying to get our friends out," he said.

"Sounds like something Conny would do."

"He's changed since you last saw him," Lionel said. "He believes in God. He has the mark."

Taylor shook his head. "Not that again."

"God's after you, man," Pete said. "Your brother's no dummy. Why can't you see—"

"I don't argue that you people have something," Taylor interrupted. "I just don't think it's for me. At least not yet."

"None of us knows how long we have left," Pete said.

"Before I turn to religion, I've got a few scores to settle," Taylor said. "And the first thing I want to do is get Conrad away from the GC."

Judd told Pete and Taylor what they would do the next day.

"Doesn't sound like much of a plan," Taylor said.

"Exactly," Mark said. "We need guns, grenades, and a few snipers in position."

Judd looked at Mark. "I thought you learned your lesson with the militia," he said.

"We're not going to kill anybody. We just want to get our own people out."

Pete yawned. "We're all tired," he said. "Let's get some sleep and talk in the morning."

Judd made sure everyone had a place to sleep. As he lay down he noticed Taylor and Mark whispering.

Conrad couldn't sleep. He kept going over the plan in his head. There were things Judd didn't know, things Conrad didn't have time to explain.

Melinda and Felicia were almost bursting with glee about the prospect of getting Lionel, Vicki, and Judd. They had talked about it on the way to their tent that night.

"The commander told me they're all gonna get it tomorrow," Felicia had said. "There's no way they're going to let that Stahley girl go. And Stein is toast."

Conrad had also overheard the commander talking with another officer about the operation. The GC would have men in position overnight with the latest high-powered rifles. The commander didn't want any surprises.

Conrad needed to talk with Darrion and Mr. Stein about the plan, but he couldn't get to them. He would have to wait and hope they followed his lead the next day.

Conrad sat up and checked his gun again. He could think of only one way to get Darrion and Mr. Stein out. And he knew his plan could get him killed.

Judd awoke from a deep sleep. Pete was shaking his shoulders.

"Do you know where Taylor is?" Pete said.

Judd saw the empty spot on the ground. "Could he have gone for some firewood?"

"Not likely," Pete said. "He was pretty fired up last night once he found out where his little brother was."

Judd woke Mark up. "What were you guys talking about last night?" Judd said.

Mark looked sheepish. "How wimpy your plan is," he said. "Taylor said there's no chance of any of us getting out of there the way things stand."

"Do you know where he went?" Judd said.

Mark shook his head. "He said he might leave early. I asked to go with him. He said he'd think about it."

Judd checked both entrances but found no sign of Taylor. He pulled out the computer and figured there was only enough battery power for one more session.

Conrad's last message gave Judd the location of the GC snipers. *I'll be right next to the commander,* he wrote. *Be warned. They're not taking prisoners.*

"We're walking into a trap," Mark said.

"We have to chance it," Judd said.

Vicki spoke up. "Maybe God wants us to stop running. Maybe he wants us in one of those reeducation camps."

"Don't you understand?" Mark said.

"Conrad said they're not taking prisoners. They're going to make an example of you." He turned to Judd. "If I can get a rifle, I could pick off—"

"No!" Judd said.

Mark walked away. Judd looked at Shelly and Vicki. "You guys don't have to go," he said. "I could have Pete take you somewhere."

"I don't know what'll happen," Vicki said, "but I'm not leaving Darrion and Mr. Stein alone. I'm in."

Shelly hesitated. "I can't take it anymore," she said. "I'll take a ride."

Before they left the cave, Judd pulled a piece of paper from Ryan's packet he had found. "I found this last night," he said. "It's in Ryan's handwriting."

Judd spread the verse out on a rock. It said: *Zechariah 4:6, "It is not by force nor by strength, but by my Spirit, says the Lord Almighty."*

Mark said, "I want to do things in God's strength too, but this is like putting David in front of Goliath without a slingshot."

"You don't have to go," Judd said.

"You know I don't mean that," Mark said.

Pete stood, and the kids grew silent. "I haven't been at this long, but I know if somebody's in trouble and I can do something, I'm going. I think we should pray."

Vicki's hand was dwarfed by Pete's. One by one the others joined hands.

"God, you showed me the truth about you, and I thank you," Pete prayed. "I thank you for these brave kids who want to help their friends. Show us what to do and when to do it. Amen."

Conrad stayed close to Commander Blancka throughout the morning. Melinda and Felicia went to the church to view the progress. Reports from the site didn't sound good for the kids.

"The snipers have been in place since early this morning," Melinda radioed back. "They're hidden so well I had to have them pointed out."

A few minutes later Felicia made contact with the commander. "We've found that weird kid, Charlie," she said. "He was staying down here with a dog. What do you want us to do?"

"Get him to one of the shelters," the commander said, "and keep everyone else away from the area."

The commander rubbed his hands together and talked to his aide. "We'll let them come to us," he said. "I want no choppers, no observation of any kind. We want them to think everything's just like I said."

Vicki squinted at the sky as she climbed out of the metal pipe. Her skin had grown pale inside the cave, and it felt good to be out. The sun was blocked by dark clouds, but the natural light felt good. The kids followed Pete to the bridge and found only one motorcycle.

"Where do you think Taylor went?" Judd said.

Pete shook his head. "Can't worry about it now," he said. "Duck under here."

The kids watched the patrols on the other side. "How are we gonna get across?" Vicki said.

"Watch," Pete said.

Vicki saw a cloud of dust about a mile away. When the cloud moved closer, the roar of motorcycles echoed across the water.

"We go now," Pete said, starting his motorcycle and heading for the other side.

"Stay close to me," Judd said as he trotted across the bridge.

The patrols stopped the gang. The motorcycles revved their engines and drowned out the noise made by Pete. As he rode past, he snatched the gun out of one guard's hands and knocked the other to the ground. One bearded man picked up the gun and motioned for both guards to get on the ground.

"What are they doing?" Vicki said.

"They won't hurt them," Judd said. "They'll lock them in the guard building and take their radios until this is over."

Vicki and the others walked past the guards. Vicki counted fifteen motorcycles, each with a single rider. Most were men, but there were also three women. They were dressed in leather and wore helmets or bandannas.

"I was hoping Red would be here," Judd said.

Pete shook his head. "Still workin' on Red," he said.

Shelly climbed on a motorcycle.

"Take her to the place," Pete said.

The female rider nodded. As the two sped off, a woman stretched a gloved hand out to Vicki. "Sally," she said.

"Pleased to meet you," Vicki said.

The group roared off. Vicki felt queasy.

Conrad looked at his watch. It was a few minutes before 5:00 P.M. His hands were sweating. Thick blue-and-black clouds rolled into the area.

The commander sat on his jeep, looking through binoculars. A cloud of dust appeared on the horizon. Conrad noticed a faint rumbling.

"What in the world?" the commander said. He looked to his aide. "Find out what that is."

"Sir," the aide said, "you said no one was to—"

"Just get somebody up there!"

"Yes, sir," the aide said.

Conrad unsnapped his holster and waited. A lone figure appeared on a small hill above the church. Conrad looked at the snipers hidden behind trees and in the church rubble. They were poised to fire.

Two other figures appeared on the hill.

"There they are," Commander Blancka said. He clicked his radio. "They look unarmed, but be careful. No one fires unless I give the order. We've got them now."

ELEVEN

Darkening Skies

CONRAD watched the scene closely, wondering when to make his move. The commander lowered his binoculars and said, "Bring those two up here."

Two guards kept watch over Darrion and Mr. Stein. Conrad hurried to them and gruffly led them away by handcuffs. When they had gone a few steps, Conrad slipped a key to Mr. Stein. "Unlock them, but keep them on," Conrad whispered.

"Are we going now?" Darrion whispered.

"Not yet," Conrad said. "If you try to run, they'll be all over you."

"I don't believe they'll let us out of here alive," Mr. Stein said.

"Don't worry," Conrad said. "I still have to get you to the Meeting of the Witnesses in a couple of days."

Mr. Stein sighed. Darrion shook with fear.

"We're gonna make it, I promise," Conrad said.

The three were nearly back to the commander's position when Conrad whispered, "When I make my move, you two stay as close to me as you possibly can. Right next to me, OK?"

Darrion and Mr. Stein nodded.

Judd pointed toward the jeep. "That has to be the commander," he said.

"Where're Darrion and Mr. Stein?" Vicki said.

"There," Lionel said, as Conrad led the two into view.

The kids stood on a knoll that overlooked the church property. A black cloud hovered over them.

"If I'm right," Lionel said, "they'll have snipers around the church and—look there, behind the tree."

"Let's just hope Conrad can come through for us," Judd said.

A squeal from a loudspeaker split the air. The commander blew into the microphone and said, "Put your hands in the air and come down the hill! Nothing will happen to you."

Conrad watched Judd turn to confer with Lionel and Vicki. *Don't do it*, Conrad thought.

"Send Darrion and Mr. Stein halfway, then we'll come down," Judd said.

The commander cursed, then clicked the microphone and spoke calmly. "Now, Judd, I gave you my word nothing would happen. We're here waiting, like we said. We didn't try to find you or follow you."

"What are the snipers doing at the church and along the tree line?" Judd yelled.

The commander radioed the snipers and told them to get ready. "Fire on my command," he said.

Conrad reached for his gun. Suddenly, the sound of engines roared in the distance. Motorcycle riders encircled the three on the hill.

"I count ten cycles," someone said on the radio.

"They're not armed, sir," another said.

Conrad saw a huge man get off his cycle and say something to Judd. The engines revved, then shut off.

Judd yelled, "You said no one would try to stop us! What are your troops doing moving around behind us?"

Commander Blancka fumed. He meant to key his microphone but spoke over the loudspeaker instead. "I told you people to stay out of sight—" When he heard his voice echo, he clicked on the microphone. "Pull back! Pull back!"

"Commander, we have clear shots on all of them," a sniper said.

Conrad studied the commander's face. If the snipers started shooting it would be all over in seconds.

Lionel heard movement behind them. Mark crawled up the hill. "Cycles are ready," Mark said. "Enough for us and the three of them."

"Start them now," Judd said.

A wind kicked up and blew dirt and sand in their faces.

"Assuming we get all three," Vicki said, "where are we going?"

"Leave that to me," Pete said. "I got it covered."

Conrad reached for his gun again. The commander bit his lip. "I wanted to bring them in without this," the commander said.

"Targets are clear, sir," a sniper radioed.

"This is probably as good a time as any," the commander said. He keyed his microphone.

"No!" Conrad yelled, pulling his gun and holding it against the commander. The man was so stunned he kept the microphone on and shouted, "Graham, what is this?"

Darrion and Mr. Stein closed in on them.

"I've got a gun on the commander," Conrad said. The commander looked down and let go of the microphone. Mr. Stein slipped his handcuffs on the man.

"Hold your fire," Conrad heard a sniper say. "One of the Morale Monitors has a gun on the commander."

Vicki shielded her eyes from the wind. "What's he doing?" she said.

"It's part of the plan," Judd said. "He doesn't want to hurt him—his gun's not even loaded—but the GC don't know that."

"Bring 'em out, Conrad," Lionel coaxed.

"Everybody down," Judd said.

From the ground, Vicki saw a comical sight. Mr. Stein and Darrion held hands around Conrad and the commander. The group turned in circles as they moved toward the hill.

"Why's he doing that?" Vicki said.

"The snipers," Lionel said. "They won't want to hurt the commander, and it's harder to hit a moving target."

Conrad ripped the radio from the commander's shoulder. It was just after 5:00 P.M. but it looked like night.

"You'll pay for this, Graham," the commander said.

"We don't want to hurt you," Conrad said. "Keep moving."

Conrad heard someone running. Darrion screamed. Melinda ran at them with her gun outstretched. When she saw Conrad she yelled, "You traitor!"

A deafening roar split the sky as a helicopter rose up behind Melinda. The pilot trained his spotlight on her. The wind blew the chopper. The pilot couldn't keep it steady. Melinda fell to the ground in terror.

"We got you now!" the commander shouted. "You might get to your group, but you'll never escape the Global Community!"

The chopper, only a few feet off the ground, turned and faced the rubble of New

Hope Village Church. "Stand clear of the building," the pilot said on a loudspeaker. A missile shot from the side of the helicopter. Snipers scattered from the building as the bomb exploded, sending a plume of smoke and debris into the air.

"What in the world—?" the commander said.

The pilot turned the chopper and faced the small group. The blades beat the air above their heads. Conrad peered into the cockpit and saw the pilot give a thumbs-up and smile.

"Taylor?" Conrad said. "It's my brother!"

Taylor motioned for them to get in. With the commander still in the middle of the group, Darrion, Mr. Stein, and Conrad stepped onto the struts.

Conrad was inches from the commander's face. "You'll never get away," the commander said.

Conrad opened his gun to show it had no bullets. "We might not, but you can't say we didn't give it a good try," he said. He handed the gun to the man as the helicopter lifted off.

"Fire, fire!" the commander shouted as the door closed.

Bullets pinged off the bulletproof glass.

Judd and the others rolled away from the hilltop as bullets aimed at the helicopter whizzed past them.

"What's happening?" Vicki said.

"New plan," Judd said. "Just get ready!"

The helicopter landed just over the hill. Darrion, Mr. Stein, and Conrad scampered out.

"I'll hold them off," Taylor yelled. "Get out of here!"

Taylor lifted straight up. The wind swirled and lightning flashed above the kids.

"Here they come!" Vicki yelled.

Judd peeked over the hill and saw a wave of GC soldiers. Commander Blancka ran with handcuffs still on.

Another helicopter appeared from behind the GC troops. Taylor shot a missile into the ground before the oncoming soldiers, and they fell back. The other helicopter bore down on Taylor with its guns blazing.

Lionel tugged on Judd's arm. The two ran down the hill as an explosion rocked the earth. One of the helicopters had crashed. Judd hopped on the back of Pete's motorcycle, and they sped away.

Judd turned and saw a group of snipers

topping the hill. They knelt and aimed their rifles at the kids.

Judd gulped. *And we were almost out of here*, he thought.

But the snipers didn't fire. Instead, they ducked, put hands in the air, and fell to the ground. Judd felt something on his head, like someone was throwing gravel. Pete and the others stopped and tried to cover themselves with their motorcycles. Judd felt sharp stings on his arms, his neck, his back.

"It's hail!" Pete said.

Then the sky opened up. The hailstones grew bigger and pelted the motorcycles. They were almost the size of golf balls, falling around them and piling up like snow. Judd watched from ground level, protected by the motorcycle. The hail clanged off the gas tank and cracked the speedometer.

An orange glow encircled them. Judd thought it was lightning at first, flashing across the sky, but it wasn't. The hailstones, at least half of them, were in flames!

"What's happening?" Pete yelled.

"One of God's judgments!" Judd screamed. "I read something by Dr. Ben-Judah about an angel throwing hail and fire to the earth."

Judd saw Vicki a few yards away, huddled

under a motorcycle. Mr. Stein had pulled his shirt over his head for protection. When the flaming hail hit the ice, it sizzled, and smoke curled from the ground.

Some of the fiery hail hit trees. They burst into flames, their branches sending fire and smoke into the air. Grass caught on fire and scorched the hillside. Judd was mixed with fear and wonder. God had promised this thousands of years ago. Now it was coming true before his eyes.

Judd saw more ice fall on the blackened ground. It piled up white, then in sections began to turn red. The drops looked like paint balls exploding on the ground and spreading in all directions.

"Blood!" Judd said.

It poured from the sky. The melted hail mixed with the blood, sending rivers of red around them. Judd put a hand into the stream of red. It was thick, oozing through his fingers. He held it to his face. It even smelled like blood.

Lightning flashed and thunder shook the ground. The hail started again, this time bigger. Some were as big as softballs. The trees that had burst into flames now sizzled as the hail put out the fire.

Judd could only cover his head and pray. It was like being in a video game with thousands of fireworks falling around him. Only this wasn't a game.

The black cloud rolled on. As the last of the hail fell, the sun peeked out. Judd saw the results of the angel's judgment. The trees had turned black as ash. Bushes and shrubs were burned to a crisp. The blood and water seeped into the ground. Charred grass broke through the white and red.

Pete pushed the bike upright. Red blotches marked his face where he had driven into the first volley of hail. Judd jumped on the back of the cycle, and Pete kicked the machine to life.

They slid through the slush and blood. Mr. Stein's motorcycle wiped out. The man came up with blood dripping from his shirt.

Judd had heard the screams of the Global Community soldiers who lay unprotected as the hailstorm began. He didn't want to think about what the softball-sized hail could do to a person without any protection. He wondered if Taylor Graham had been in the helicopter that crashed.

Judd counted heads as they made their way over the wet earth. The Young Trib Force was alive, at least for the moment.

Judd glanced back to see if Commander Blancka and the others would give chase. The motorcycles topped a hill and looked down on the scene. Several soldiers lay lifeless in the red earth. The charred remains of a GC copter lay smoldering nearby.

Pete gunned the engine and raced away. Moments later Judd heard the roar of rotor blades. He held on to the motorcycle and prayed.

TWELVE

The Choices Ahead

JUDD held on as Pete drove recklessly through the blood and slush. A few minutes after the sun came out, most of the hail and blood had dissolved into the ground. A helicopter passed nearby. Judd guessed the pilot had lost the bikers in the woods. He glanced at Conrad. The boy looked grim.

Pete found a main road and picked up speed. They passed abandoned cars with broken windshields. A crater had opened in the middle of the road. The remains of an exploded fuel truck lay in the bottom of the hole.

They drove through the crater and on the other side saw a helicopter coming right for them. Pete stopped. The aircraft was pocked with dents from the hail.

To Judd's surprise, the helicopter landed and Taylor Graham stepped out. He gave a thumbs-up to the group. "Almost out of fuel," he said. "Think you could give me a ride?"

Pete motioned for one of the single riders to come forward. As he did, Taylor fired up the chopper and perched it on the side of an embankment by the road. Taylor left the rotors going and stepped out. The rotors slowed, and then the black craft tipped forward and fell into the ravine. A fiery explosion shook the earth.

"Better leave before they see that smoke," Taylor said.

Vicki was glad Conrad's brother was safe. She didn't like it that he had tried to kill the commander and the others, but he had gotten Darrion, Mr. Stein, and Conrad out alive.

Vicki held tight to the motorcycle driver. She kept looking over her shoulder, thinking the GC would be right behind them.

They drove without resting, the wind in their faces. When night fell, the motorcycles looked eerie with their headlights piercing the darkness. Vicki was exhausted when they finally reached a gas station. The manager came outside with a gun, then grinned at Pete.

"Don't park out here, bring them on in," the man said.

The kids and Mr. Stein went inside while the others pulled their motorcycles into the garage. Shelly had prepared hot chocolate and sandwiches. The kids ate hungrily.

"Boyd Walker," the man said, extending a hand to each of the kids. He pointed at Judd. "This young fellow and Pete helped me out in more ways than one."

Along with grease stains, Vicki saw that the man had the mark of a true believer on his forehead.

Boyd told the story again of how Pete had saved his station from the motorcycle gang. Then Pete had returned and told him the truth about Christ's return. "I been readin' that rabbi on the Internet," Boyd said. "Got a computer in the back."

Vicki noticed that Conrad and Taylor Graham were in a heated discussion outside.

"That's not how we do things," Conrad said. "How many did you kill to get that bird from the GC?"

"I saved your tail back there," Taylor said. "A simple thank-you would be nice. Besides, I gave those guys warning before I shot."

Conrad shook his head. "I'm glad you're alive. But you have to stop trying to get revenge against the GC and start listening to what I'm saying."

"Like I told the others, I don't have time for religion right now."

Boyd had given Mr. Stein a T-shirt to replace the bloodstained one. Mr. Stein embraced Vicki. "I didn't think I would ever see you again," he said. "I still have so many questions, but Rabbi Ben-Judah is answering them now."

"Chaya would be so happy," Vicki said.

Mr. Stein blinked tears away. "I can only tell you how sorry I am," he said. "God has forgiven me for my hard heart. I know one day I will see Chaya and Judith again."

"Conrad said you're pretty set on going to Israel," Vicki said.

"The meeting is this weekend," Mr. Stein said. "I'm afraid I'll have to watch it on the Net like the rest of the world."

Vicki thought about Phoenix. It would have been impossible to bring him with them, even if she had found him. But she still felt guilty not keeping her promise to Ryan.

Lionel found Boyd's tiny black-and-white television and tuned in a station. Darrion sat beside him with a cold drink. "I can't wait to see what kind of spin Carpathia's newsmen put on what's happened!" she said.

The news anchor looked flustered, as if he had witnessed the hail and didn't believe what he was reading. The anchor gave staggering statistics about the amount of hail the area received in the few minutes the storm raged. "But Illinois was not the only area hit. In fact, this seems to have happened worldwide at the exact same time."

"So how do you explain it?" Lionel said to the TV.

The anchor introduced an expert who said the event was a "one-time occurrence" and was easily explained as an "atmospheric disturbance."

Darrion shook her head. "Yeah, and it definitely did not have anything to do with God or with his judgment of the earth."

"As many of you saw earlier, Potentate Nicolae Carpathia responded to this world crisis with decisive action," the news anchor said. "He held a news conference less than an hour ago in which he outlined the Global Community response."

Nicolae was dressed casually, as if he had strolled in from a dinner party to answer questions. But Lionel could tell the man was concerned. If he had been reading Dr. Ben-Judah's Web site as Pavel said he had, he knew this was no fluke. This was God speaking in a forceful way.

"Because of the momentary disruption in communications, I have called a halt to all travel. This means the meeting scheduled in Israel that I had approved will have to be rescheduled."

"How convenient," Darrion said.

"Citizens of the Global Community should not be alarmed," Carpathia continued. "We have everything under control, and the effects of this storm should not hinder us as we move forward in our quest for a better world."

"So if it's no problem," Lionel said, "why does he have to postpone the Meeting of the Witnesses?"

The news shifted to local effects of the storm. Video showed traffic snarls and streets filled with hail. The anchor referred to the "sticky red substance" but never called it blood. He said a few fires were also reported.

"Look!" Darrion shouted. Bikers gathered from around the station.

A shot of a downed GC helicopter flashed on the screen. Several GC soldiers lay facedown in a field near New Hope Village Church.

"At the time of the storm," the anchor continued, "the Global Community was conducting a training exercise in Mount Prospect."

"Training exercise!" Lionel yelled.

"Seven soldiers were killed by the hailstorm, and a dozen others were treated for fractures and burns at a local shelter. The leader of the exercise, Commander Terrel Blancka, has reportedly been reprimanded and will be given another assignment."

"You know the real reason they're upset with him," Darrion said.

"Yeah," Lionel said. "He let us get away."

Judd found the laptop in the saddlebag of Pete's motorcycle. It had taken a beating from the hail but still worked. He hooked it up beside Boyd's ancient machine and logged on to the Net.

"That thing's got some speed," Boyd said, admiring the laptop.

The list of forwarded E-mails from Tsion was growing. Now that they were away from the GC, Judd thought he might have a chance to answer some of them.

Judd let out a whoop and yelled for Mark.

"What's up?" Mark said.

"It's from John," Judd said.

John's message was short. It read, *If you get*

this E-mail, please respond. If you've seen any of my friends or family, please report.

Judd quickly wrote and gave Boyd's phone number. He sent a second E-mail detailing their flight from the Global Community. He sent the second message and logged off. The phone rang a few seconds later.

"Yeah, he's right here," Boyd said, handing the phone to Judd.

It was John. "I've been trying to call since I saw your first E-mail," he said. "Did everybody make it OK?"

"Ryan's gone," Judd said.

John didn't speak.

"And you knew Chaya Stein. She was killed in the quake too."

"What about Mark?" John said.

Judd handed the phone to Mark. The two talked a few minutes and then Judd got back on the line. "Give us the update," he said.

"You won't believe it," John said. "The quake hit in the middle of classes at college. I saw the lights shake and remembered what Tsion said. I made it out the window before the whole building came down.

"Then everything went crazy. I helped pull bodies out of buildings and get help to the injured. The GC showed up a couple days later looking for anyone who could walk.

There's a naval base on the coast, and some of their guys didn't make it."

"You volunteered?" Judd said.

"You don't volunteer with the GC," John said. "I said I was a first-year engineering student, and they told me to get in the truck. I didn't have a choice."

"Where are you now?" Judd said.

"I'm finishing up training," John said. "They put me in communications. We're pulling out tomorrow for the Atlantic."

"You're right," Judd said. "I don't believe it."

"The good news is I have access to everything," John said. "We get orders and reports from New Babylon just about every day. Plus, I saw your picture, which was sent from Chicago yesterday."

"A picture?" Judd said.

"More like a wanted poster," John said. "They had mug shots of you, Vicki, and Lionel."

"Have you heard the reports about what happened?" Judd said.

"You mean the training exercise?" John laughed. "The report I get is that the head guy, Blancka, has been demoted from his Morale Monitor position. They don't even know whether they'll continue the program or not."

When he was finished with John, Judd called a meeting of the Young Trib Force. Pete and a few of the other bikers sat in, along with Boyd.

"I have a message from Tsion I want to read," Judd said, "but first, I have to say something. We're wanted by the GC. They know about Darrion, Vicki, Lionel, Mr. Stein, and me. We have to make a choice. Do we stay together? And when the GC school starts, should we attend? Where do we go?"

Mark raised a hand.

"If it's OK," Judd said, "I'd like you all to sleep on it, make some notes, and be ready to talk tomorrow."

Judd opened Tsion's E-mail and read it.

We serve a great God who delivers his children. I have been praying for you since I heard of your difficulty, and will continue to pray.

I am going to Israel as soon as possible. Eli and Moishe confirmed that the time is right. The other day Eli said, "Woe unto him who sits on the throne of this earth. Should he dare stand in the way of God's sealed and anointed witnesses, twelve thousand from each of the twelve tribes making a pilgrimage here for the purpose of preparation, he shall surely suffer for it."

Then Moishe said, "Yea, any attempt to impede the moving of God among the sealed will cause your plants to wither and die, rain to remain in the clouds, and your water—all of it—to turn to blood! The Lord of hosts hath sworn, saying, 'Surely, as I have thought, so it shall come to pass, and as I have purposed, so it shall stand!'"

This lets me know the time is close. The first of the seven angels have sounded their judgments with fiery hail and blood which burned a third of the trees and all green grass.

Next to come is the second angel, which brings with it a great mountain burning with fire. This will turn a third of the earth's water to blood, kill a third of the living creatures in the sea, and sink a third of the ships.

The third angel's trumpet sound will result in a great star falling from heaven, burning like a torch. It will bring disaster with it, and many will die.

I tell you this not to scare you, but to prepare you for what is ahead. Be bold.

You may be asked to give your life. Ryan and Chaya already have.

Judd paused. Mr. Stein wept. Judd felt the emotion well up. He turned to the screen to keep from crying himself, and he read:

Wherever you are, I encourage you to think of the great soul harvest before us. I wish I had believed before the Rapture, but I rejoice in the opportunity before us. Many will become believers in Jesus in the next few months.

Be careful. The next judgments may come soon. May God help you make right decisions as you seek to lead others to the truth.

ABOUT THE AUTHORS

Jerry B. Jenkins (www.jerryjenkins.com) is the writer of the Left Behind series. He is author of more than one hundred books, of which eleven have reached the *New York Times* best-seller list. Former vice president for publishing for the Moody Bible Institute of Chicago, he also served many years as editor of *Moody* magazine and is now Moody's writer-at-large.

His writing has appeared in publications as varied as *Reader's Digest, Parade,* in-flight magazines, and many Christian periodicals. He has written books in four genres: biography, marriage and family, fiction for children, and fiction for adults.

Jenkins's biographies include books with Hank Aaron, Bill Gaither, Luis Palau, Walter Payton, Orel Hershiser, Nolan Ryan, Brett Butler, and Billy Graham, among many others.

Seven of his apocalyptic novels—*Left Behind, Tribulation Force, Nicolae, Soul Harvest, Apollyon, Assassins,* and *The Indwelling*—have appeared on the Christian Booksellers Association's best-selling fiction list and the *Publishers Weekly* religion best-seller list. *Left Behind* was nominated for Book of the Year by the Evangelical Christian Publishers Association in 1997, 1998, 1999, and 2000. *The Indwelling* was number one on the *New York Times* best-seller list for four consecutive weeks.

As a marriage and family author and speaker, Jenkins has been a frequent guest on Dr. James Dobson's *Focus on the Family* radio program.

Jerry is also the writer of the nationally syndicated sports story comic strip *Gil Thorp,* distributed to newspapers across the United States by Tribune Media Services.

Jerry and his wife, Dianna, live in Colorado.

Dr. **Tim LaHaye** (www.timlahaye.com), who conceived the idea of fictionalizing an account of the Rapture and the Tribulation, is a noted author, minister, and nationally recognized speaker on Bible prophecy. He is the founder of both Tim LaHaye Ministries and The Pre-Trib Research Center. Presently Dr. LaHaye speaks at many of the major Bible prophecy conferences in the U.S. and Canada, where his nine current prophecy books are very popular.

Dr. LaHaye holds a doctor of ministry degree from Western Theological Seminary and the doctor of literature degree from Liberty University. For twenty-five years he pastored one of the nation's outstanding churches in San Diego, which grew to three locations. It was during that time that he founded two accredited Christian high schools, a Christian school system of ten schools, and Christian Heritage College.

Dr. LaHaye has written over forty books, with over 30 million copies in print in thirty-three languages. He has written books on a wide variety of subjects, such as family life, temperaments, and Bible prophecy. His current fiction works, written with Jerry Jenkins—*Left Behind, Tribulation Force, Nicolae, Soul Harvest, Apollyon, Assassins,* and *The Indwelling*—have all reached number one on the Christian best-seller charts. Other works by Dr. LaHaye are *Spirit-Controlled Temperament; How to Be Happy Though Married; Revelation Unveiled; Understanding the Last Days; Rapture under Attack; Are We Living in the End Times?;* and the youth fiction series Left Behind: The Kids.

He is the father of four grown children and grandfather of nine. Snow skiing, waterskiing, motorcycling, golfing, vacationing with family, and jogging are among his leisure activities.

The Future Is Clear

In one shocking moment, millions around the globe disappear. Those left behind face an uncertain future—especially the four kids who now find themselves alone.

Best-selling authors Jerry B. Jenkins and Tim LaHaye present the Rapture and Tribulation through the eyes of four friends—Judd, Vicki, Lionel, and Ryan. As the world falls in around them, they band together to find faith and fight the evil forces that threaten their lives.

#1: The Vanishings Four friends face Earth's last days together.

#2: Second Chance The kids search for the truth.

#3: Through the Flames The kids risk their lives.

#4: Facing the Future The kids prepare for battle.

#5: Nicolae High The Young Trib Force goes back to school.

#6: The Underground The Young Trib Force fights back.

#7: Busted! The Young Trib Force faces pressure.

#8: Death Strike The Young Trib Force faces war.

#9: The Search The struggle to survive.

#10: On the Run The Young Trib Force faces danger.

BOOKS #16 AND #17 COMING SOON!